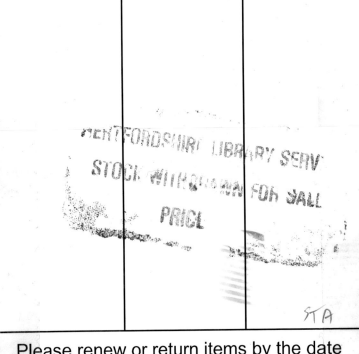

Please renew or return items by the date
shown on your receipt

www.hertfordshire.gov.uk/libraries

Renewals and enquiries: 0300 123 4049

Textphone for hearing or 0300 123 4041
speech impaired users:

L32 11.1

Hertfordshire

D1142625

HIS SHOCK MARRIAGE IN GREECE

JANE PORTER

MILLS & BOON

First Published in Great Britain 2019
by Mills & Boon, an imprint of HarperCollins*Publishers*
1 London Bridge Street, London, SE1 9GF

© 2019 Jane Porter

ISBN: 978-0-263-27075-4

MIX
Paper from
responsible sources
FSC™ C007454

This book is produced from independently certified FSC™ paper
to ensure responsible forest management.
For more information visit www.harpercollins.co.uk/green.

Printed and bound in Spain
by CPI, Barcelona

PROLOGUE

KASSIANI DUKAS TRIED to sit very still on the white slip-covered upholstered sofa in the corner of the expansive villa's living room, not wanting to draw attention to herself as it would only lead to trouble.

She'd done nothing wrong but her father was furious and the last thing she wanted was him to turn on her.

Things were bad, though. Elexis was gone. Kassiani's older sister was to marry Damen Alexopoulos tomorrow but Elexis had mysteriously disappeared in the night, managing to sneak away from the estate on the Athenian Riviera before flying out of Athens with friends more than willing to whisk her away from a wedding—and marriage— she'd never wanted.

And now her father was about to break the news to her groom, powerful Greek shipping tycoon Damen Alexopoulos, a man everyone knew to be brilliant, ambitious and dangerous if crossed.

He'd just been crossed.

She shuddered as her father, Kristopher, paced the gleaming marble floor, hands knotted behind his back, his complexion ashen. Nothing good would come of Elexis's disappearance.

Footsteps rang in the hall. Kassiani sat taller on the corner sofa. Kristopher stopped his frenetic pacing.

Damen Alexopoulos entered the villa's living room, stealing Kassiani's breath. She'd seen him before, on the night of Elexis's engagement, but she hadn't actually talked to him. It had been a party for others—very public, very extravagant with Elexis and Damen spending maybe just thirty minutes together—before he'd flown out, returning to Greece. He wasn't classically handsome, but he had piercing hazel eyes, strong, arresting features and a full, firm mouth that fascinated her. He was also taller than she remembered, and broader through the shoulders, with a muscular chest and narrow waist and long lean legs.

Kass had never understood why Elexis hadn't found him attractive, because as Greek men went, he was truly a remarkable specimen, but then her sister tended to prefer the up-and-coming models and actors who fawned all over her, each of those young, pretty males hoping to benefit from her wealth and fame.

"I was told you wanted to see me," Damen said, his voice deep with a hint of a rasp that made the fine hair on Kassiani's nape rise while her insides did a peculiar quiver.

"Good morning, Damen," her father said with forced cheer. "It's a beautiful morning here in Sousin."

A small muscle pulled in Damen's hard jaw. Kassiani could tell he found her father annoying. That didn't bode well for what was to come.

"It is always beautiful here," Damen answered. "But I ended an important meeting to see you, having been told there was an emergency."

Irritation and impatience made the rasp in his voice more pronounced, and his English more accented. It was clear he hadn't learned English as a boy. Or at least, he hadn't become fluent as a boy.

"An emergency? No," Kristopher replied, smiling. "I wouldn't call it that. I'm sorry you had to rush here, worrying."

The muscle in Damen's jaw worked again. It was clear he

was fighting to hang on to his temper. "I don't worry, and I don't rush. But I am now here. Why was I summoned?"

Kassiani drew back in the corner of the sofa, as if she could make herself smaller. Not easy as she was a big girl… not tall like her sister, but rather, big boned, with even bigger curves—hips, breasts and the sort of generous backside that was fashionable if paired with a tiny waist. But Kassiani's waist wasn't spectacularly tiny. Her stomach wasn't flat. Her thighs touched. Unlike her older sister, Kassiani didn't have an Instagram account. She didn't take selfies. She avoided photos at all cost.

Unlike stunning, photogenic Elexis, Kass didn't photograph well. Nor was she part of high society's inner circle. She didn't travel on private jet planes, or party in Las Vegas, the Caribbean or Mediterranean.

If her last name hadn't been Dukas, she would have been incredibly ordinary. If her father wasn't one of the richest Greeks in America, she would have been forgotten. Invisible.

Over the years Kass had come to wish she really was invisible as invisible was far better than being visible and pitied. Visible and scorned. Visible and rejected. And not just rejected by superficial socialites and quasi-celebrities, but rejected by your own family.

Her father had never shown the least bit of interest in her, and why should he when he had everything he needed in his son and heir, Barnabas, and beautiful Elexis, who'd charmed him from birth with her big dark eyes and winsome pout?

Kass had never been a charming child. Family lore depicted her as silent and sullen, and impossibly stubborn. She reportedly scowled at guests, refusing to make small talk with her father's important guests. She wouldn't play the piano or sing, or bat her eyelashes at the visiting Greek dignitaries. Instead, Kass wanted to discuss politics with her father's friends. Even at four and five she was fascinated by economics. She'd make predictions about the future of the shipping industry, and her audacity horrified her father. It didn't matter that she read beyond her years. It didn't matter that she excelled in math. Good Greek girls didn't weigh in on national matters, or international policies and economics. Good Greek girls grew up and made good marriages with suitable Greek men and produced the next generation. That was their responsibility. That was their value. Nothing else.

It wasn't long before Kassiani wasn't included in the family parties. She wasn't asked to dress up and come downstairs. She wasn't invited to the dinners and weddings and reunions. She became the forgotten Dukas.

"I appreciate you coming straightaway," Kristopher said, still smiling, but less broadly. "I hate disturbing you but we have a problem."

Kassiani's father was a shipping tycoon like Damen, but Greek American, having been born and raised in San Francisco. She knew he was nervous, but his voice didn't betray it. If anything, he sounded positive and optimistic. She was glad. One couldn't ever betray fear in contract negotiations, and the merger of Dukas Shipping with the Alexopoulos empire through marriage of Damen and Elexis was the ultimate business transaction. A transaction that was now in jeopardy.

Her stomach knotted and cramped. There was no way her father could ever pay Damen back for the money he'd invested in the Dukas ships and ports. Her father lacked the means. The business and family were perpetually cash-strapped. It was why her father had sought out the merger five years ago. Dukas Shipping would fold without an investor. Damen had been the investor. He'd upheld his end of the deal, but now Kristopher had to inform Damen that the Dukases hadn't kept their side of the bargain.

Nauseous, Kassiani looked out the villa window, seeking the view beyond. The sun reflected brilliantly off the villa's whitewashed walls and bounced in cheerful rays off the water, the Aegean Sea so much brighter—a vibrant liquid turquoise—than the murky blue of the Pacific Ocean near her home in San Francisco.

"I'm not certain I understand," Damen answered just as pleasantly, both men employing the same friendly tone, but Kassiani knew this was just a prelude to battle.

Boxers touched gloves before a bout. Wrestlers bowed before a match. Soccer players shook hands.

Her father and Damen were already fencing.

She glanced from her father to Damen. No, he didn't look like a tycoon. He was too fit, too physically imposing. His skin was bronzed, and he had the toned, taut look of a man who worked in the shipyards, not at a desk. But it was his profile that held her attention, his features as chiseled and hard as the rest of him, the forehead high, cheekbones prominent, nose decidedly thick at the bridge, as if broken more than once.

He was a fighter, she thought, and he wouldn't take her father's news sitting down, which only made Kassiani even more grateful she was seated, tucked into a corner sofa.

"Elexis is gone." Kristopher delivered the news bluntly, before adding, "I'm hoping to have her back soon, we just need—"

"I'm sorry. I must stop you there, Dukas." Damen's voice dropped, the rasp softening into almost a caress. "We don't have a problem. *You* have a problem."

Kristopher held his position but his ashen complexion seemed to pale yet again. "I'm aware of that, but I thought we should notify guests while there is time."

"There is no canceling the wedding. There will be no broken promises. There will be no public humiliation. Is that understood?"

"But—"

"You promised me the best daughter five years ago. I expect you to deliver."

The best daughter. Kassiani's eyes stung and she bit into her lower lip to hold back the hurt and shame.

She hadn't thought she'd made a sound but suddenly Damen looked at her. His expression was shuttered, his black lashes framing intense, dark eyes. She could read nothing in his face and yet somehow that brief glance skewered her, intensifying her pain.

She was not the best daughter. She would never be the best daughter, not as long as she remained a Dukas.

Damen turned back to her father and his firm full lips curved ever so slightly at the corner, a contemptuous light in his gray eyes. "I will see you tomorrow at the church," he said. "With my bride."

And then he walked out.

CHAPTER ONE

IT WAS A perfect day for a May wedding on the Greek Riviera.

The sky was an endless, azure blue with just a smattering of puffy white clouds. The sun reflected brightly off the thick walls of the villa's tiny whitewashed chapel, glazing the tiled roof, while the Aegean Sea and the Temple of Poseidon shimmered in the background. The temperature was perfect as well, comfortable and warm, without being hot, or humid.

Ordinarily, a bride would be ecstatic at such perfect conditions, but Kassiani was no ordinary bride. She was not even supposed to *be* the bride.

Today was her sister's wedding, with the ceremony and reception to take place at Damen's historic seaside villa in Sounio, but early this morning Kristopher Dukas made the drastic decision to swap brides on the unsuspecting bridegroom, thus Kassiani now stood outside the villa chapel's wooden door, waiting her cue to enter, while knots in her stomach exploded, turning into frantic butterflies.

There was a huge possibility this would not end well. She fully expected the groom to walk out on her in the middle of the service, abandoning her in the tiny church.

The bridegroom was not a fool.

The bridegroom was one of the most powerful men in the world, and he would not like being duped.

Kassiani was not in the habit of duping men, either.

She was the youngest Dukas. The least remarkable in

every way. But when cornered by her father this morning, she'd agreed to his plan and would marry Damen Alexopoulos not because it would save her father's hide, but it'd save hers, as well.

Marriage to Damen would be her way out. She'd escape her father's house. She'd escape her father's control. *And* she'd come into the trust her late aunt had established for her, a trust that would give her some measure of freedom and financial control.

It was worth noting, too, that the wedding today would mean she had actually accomplished something significant in her father's eyes. Even if it meant she was giving up one controlling male for another, because at twenty-three, she was ready to do something, and be someone other than plain, dumpy, uninspiring Kassiani Dukas.

Marrying the fabulously wealthy shipping tycoon Damen Alexopoulos wouldn't change the way she looked, but it would change the way people thought of her, and spoke of her. It would force them to recognize her as someone of consequence, pathetic as that was.

The harpist played within the church, and her father—short, stout, with thick salt-and-pepper hair—gestured impatiently for her. Kassiani suppressed a sigh. Her father really didn't like her. As a little girl she'd never understood his coldness, because he absolutely doted on Elexis, but as she grew up and came to understand the world, she was able to put the pieces together.

Kristopher was not a handsome man, and he wanted to be liked. Respected. Having money was just one way to be respected. Having beautiful children was another. And while Elexis was their late mother's clone—their mother, having been a successful model before she'd given up her career to marry the Greek American shipping magnate—Kassiani unfortunately favored her father, inheriting both his build and his strong jaw. Not what a woman wanted when her mother had been a famous model.

Kassiani exhaled in a depressing whoosh. These thoughts were not helping. Her self-esteem—never strong—was plummeting by the moment. And then her father snapped his fingers.

It seemed it was time.

The butterflies returned and her hand trembled as she took her father's arm. He paused to adjust her heavy lace veil, better cloaking her face.

Kassiani felt utterly terrified, and yet also strangely calm. Once they stepped into the chapel, there would be no turning back. Elexis had let her father down. Elexis had let the entire family down. Kass would do no such thing.

For once she could do something to benefit her father's vast shipping business. She'd wanted to work for Dukas Shipping since she was in second grade. She'd even studied business and international law at Stanford so she'd be of value, but her father had rebuffed her, refusing to hire her, or even listen to her ideas. He was painfully old-fashioned, believing a woman's value was at home, producing heirs, and preferably male heirs.

After twenty-three years of being useless, after twenty-three years of being an embarrassment, she was aiding her father, significantly aiding him by saving him from bankruptcy and all the ensuing humiliation and shame.

Empowered, Kassiani drew a breath, lifted her chin and took her first step into the four-hundred-year-old Greek Orthodox church. It took her eyes a moment to adjust to the cool, dark interior, and then she spotted the groom before her. It really was a tiny chapel, with just five rows of pews on either side of the narrow aisle.

Damen Michael Alexopoulos stood at the front, just before the altar and priest. Once Kassiani spotted her future husband, she couldn't look away. Dressed in a severe black suit, he looked even more intimidating than he had yesterday in the villa suite. She didn't know if it was his height, or the width of his shoulders, but there was a dangerous stillness about him now that made the air catch in her throat.

Was he suspicious?

Had he already figured out she wasn't the right bride?

Kass was so heavily veiled that she could barely see through the thick white lace, but he was no fool and it wouldn't take much to assess her size and shape and realize that there was no way she was Elexis, of Instagram fame. Elexis was opposite Kass in every way imaginable. Even wearing treacherously high heels, Kassiani remained short, her plump figure wrapped in the tightest of undergarments, including the old-fashioned corset necessary to make Elexis's dress fit, and that was *after* the dress had been altered to include additional panels and a dramatically shortened hem.

"He knows," she said under her breath.

"He doesn't," her father gritted. "And it's too late for second thoughts. You cannot fail me."

A lump filled her throat. She wouldn't. She couldn't.

She clenched his arm and kept her chin high. The only way through challenging times was to go through them. There would be no retreat. There would be no panicking. She would make this work. She would find a way to please her husband. She would bring the two families together. And it would be her, Petra Kassiani, who did it, not Elexis, and not her playboy brother, Barnabas, who had so little familial love that he hadn't even bothered to show up for the wedding.

She could do this. She could.

The real question was, would he?

* * *

Damen knew the moment Kristopher Dukas entered the chapel with his daughter that it was the wrong daughter.

He watched them process—portly Kristopher with his heavily veiled daughter teetering in her heels—unable to believe the American's audacity.

It seemed that once again Kristopher took the easy way out. Instead of retrieving the wayward Elexis, Kristopher had simply swapped daughters, substituting the youngest for the eldest.

Who did that?

What kind of man treated his daughters like cattle?

Damen felt a jolt—shock, disbelief—as Kristopher placed his younger daughter's hand in his, handing her over at the altar, clearly the sacrificial lamb. Even Damen, who was ruthless in business, knew the difference between dishonesty and betrayal. And this was a betrayal.

It's not that he needed a beauty queen for a bride, but this younger daughter wasn't Elexis and he'd chosen Elexis for a reason.

Gleaming, polished, ambitious Elexis Dukas suited him in looks and temperament. She'd hold her own socially, and she'd be an accomplished hostess, things he knew he needed in a wife because he detested social engagements and refused to be part of any dog and pony show. Elexis loved the spotlight. She loved attention. She could easily represent them at important functions and no one would miss him. Why would they, when they had her?

He felt no affection for Elexis, but she was the one he wanted, and he hadn't proposed to her without knowing exactly what he was getting in a wife—both strengths and weaknesses. Elexis led an enviable lifestyle. She traveled with the jet set. She partied at all the best clubs. She wore the best clothes, sitting in the front rows of the biggest fashion shows. Her life was one photo opportunity after another, but he'd let her carry on as she always had during their engagement, aware that once she became his wife, she'd settle down and become a proper wife.

He needed a proper wife, one who understood her place in his world, and wouldn't make emotional demands. He didn't do emotions. And he didn't tolerate demands.

But now Elexis was gone and there was a very different Dukas at his side and it suddenly crossed Damen's mind that perhaps this had been Kristopher's plan from the beginning. Perhaps Elexis had never intended to marry him? Perhaps Kristopher had never planned on giving his beloved Elexis to Damen?

Perhaps Kristopher had always intended on dumping his youngest, the one he casually referred to as the Dukas Ugly Duckling, on him.

He should walk out now.

And just when he was about to drop the Ugly Duckling's hand, she lifted her face, her dark gaze finding his through her veil, and whispered, "I'm sorry."

They signed the registry in the chapel's antechamber. Damen gritted his teeth, angry beyond measure as it struck him that the worst part of this—no, not the worst but yet another negative among negatives—was that he didn't even know his new wife's name. "So who have I married, if not Elexis?" he ground out as the priest handed him a pen.

Her long lace veil had been folded back on the top of her head and she glanced at him but looked away, unable to hold his furious gaze. He felt a tightness in his chest as her ridiculously long black lashes dropped, concealing her eyes.

"Kassiani," she said huskily.

He felt angrier by the moment. His fingers itched to

smash something hard—like the narrow table, or the nearest stone wall. "That wasn't the name in the ceremony."

"No, the priest used my legal first name, Petra, but no one calls me Petra. I'm either Kass or Kassiani."

He ground his teeth together, not just upset with her, but with himself for not having walked out of the service when he could. Why had he let her apology sway him? Why had her whispered words kept him from leaving her there at the altar?

He didn't know the answers to any of those questions, and he wasn't in the frame of mind to sort it out. "Do not think this is over," he said curtly after signing his name and handing the pen to her.

She looked up at him as she accepted the pen, a faint line between her arched eyebrows, expression troubled. "I don't."

"Was this always the plan, to swap sisters on the unsuspecting groom?"

Color suffused her pale cheeks. "No."

"Don't take this the wrong way, but I didn't want you."

The pink color swiftly faded from her face. Her full lips compressed as she drew a slow breath and then she managed an unsteady laugh. "Understood."

"I'm not trying to be offensive."

She lifted her chin and met his gaze then, her eyes locking with his. "No offense taken."

In any other circumstances, he thought he would have liked her. She was direct and smart and articulate. But this wasn't a casual conversation. He'd just been played and he wasn't in the most charitable frame of mind. "I'm not one to forgive and forget."

He saw a shadow pass across her face, and he almost felt sorry for her, but then the shadow disappeared, leaving her expression calm and composed. "And as you can see, I'm not one to pass up a slice of cake, or a bit of a chocolate." Then she leaned over the registry and added her name, her long lace veil spilling across her shoulder in a waterfall of white. When she'd finished, she straightened and squared her shoulders and handed back the pen. "It seems we all have our crosses to bear."

He didn't know if it was her words, or her ridiculous bravado, but he felt a rush of intense emotion—emotion he didn't welcome—and drew her hard against him, tilting her chin back with one hand before covering her mouth, capturing it with his. She was petite, barely reaching his shoulder, and impossibly warm and soft, which made his kiss harder, and fiercer. It wasn't the kiss a man should give his young bride, but nothing about this wedding was right.

Upstairs in the luxurious villa bedroom Kassiani had dressed in earlier, she walked back and forth, chewing on a knuckle, trying to calm herself.

He didn't want her, and he didn't like her, and she had a feeling this could all still fall apart any moment.

The vows wouldn't hold, not unless the marriage was consummated, and she couldn't imagine him taking her to his bed right now. Quite frankly, she didn't want to be in his bed, either, and she shuddered remembering his cold-ness as he'd told her he didn't forgive and forget.

She didn't doubt him.

Which was why she was here in the bedroom, hiding. She'd lost her nerve. Somehow she'd found the necessary courage this morning to take Elexis's place for the cere-mony, but that courage was gone.

Thank God the ceremony had been small and private. No one but the immediate family attended. However, the reception was large, with hundreds of guests flying in from all over the world to witness the marriage of Elexis Dukas and Damen Alexopoulos.

Kassiani stopped pacing to double over, wanting to throw up as she imagined appearing at the reception. The guests would laugh when they saw her. It was one thing to be Elexis in private, hidden beneath layers of thick lace. It was another to be Elexis in front of those who knew her sister best.

Kass couldn't imagine joining Damen on the terrace for dinner, or dancing, or cutting of the cake. She'd convinced herself she could do this—but she'd thought only about the ceremony and vows. She hadn't taken in the terror of appearing in public as his new wife.

His wife.

Kassiani's legs buckled and she dropped onto the edge of the bed, her full skirts billowing up around her, her feet aching from her stupid shoes.

What had she done?

She was wiping away tears when her bedroom door suddenly opened and Damen entered her room.

He hadn't even knocked. He'd simply barged in.

Her head jerked up, her lips parting in surprise, but she uttered no protest. His fierce expression silenced anything she might have said.

She waited for him to speak.

He didn't.

He simply stared at her, and the silence was unbearable. A tremor coursed through her.

Time slowed to a crawl. The seconds felt like minutes. She tried to meet his gaze but his scathing look of contempt was more than she could endure in that moment. "Please say something," she finally murmured.

"Our guests have been waiting."

Again she pictured the stone terrace filled with linen-draped tables and gleaming candelabras. The reception was a sophisticated palette of cream, bisque and white and Kassiani did not belong there. It wasn't her wedding. They weren't her guests. This wasn't her party. "I couldn't go down."

"Am I to bring the guests up to you?"

"No. Please don't."

"Do you want to be carried down?"

"No." She couldn't look at him. Her eyes burned. What had seemed so brave and necessary this morning now seemed like the worst idea imaginable.

"It's a little late to turn coward."

She hung her head. "I agree."

Silence stretched. The room was so quiet she could hear his low, irritated exhale. "If you're expecting sympathy—"

"I'm not."

"Good. This is your own fault."

She started to speak, but then closed her mouth, pressing her lips together. He was right, of course. How could she argue the point?

"You can't just sit up here all night," he added after a moment.

She plucked at a pearl embroidered into the skirt of her gown. "I'm not much of a party person. I never have been."

"Even if it's your own wedding?"

"As we both know, it wasn't supposed to be."

"Therein lies the problem."

She briefly met his gaze, her breath catching in her throat before she swiftly averted her head, blood rushing to her cheeks.

He made her so nervous. He was nothing like her father or brother. He was nothing like anyone she'd ever known before.

"How did you think this would go?" he asked, his tone shifting, less harsh, almost mild.

The change in tone surprised her, but still she couldn't speak.

Kassiani bit her lip, unable to answer.

"Truthfully," he prompted.

Her shoulders twisted. She hated this helpless, pathetic feeling. She hated feeling like a failure. She hadn't married him to be a failure. "I didn't think about the reception and the guests. To be honest, this part didn't even cross my mind. It was just the ceremony…and then…" She drew a quick breath and lifted her head, her eyes meeting his. "…the rest."

"And what was the rest?"

"Being a proper wife." She could see from the cynical glint in his eyes that he didn't believe her. "I understand what wives do. Your comfort is my responsibility—"

"Your father told you this?"

"I'm a Greek woman. I know what Greek men expect."

There was something in his dark, speculative gaze that made her skin prickle and her pulse lurch, and she didn't know how to manage so many new and strange feelings at the same time.

"Go on, then."

She swallowed hard, trying not to betray just how nervous she felt. "Besides taking care of you, I'm to manage your home…or homes. I'm to provide you with children. And I understand and accept those responsibilities."

"It seems one of the Dukas daughters is dutiful, then."

"Elexis and I have different strengths."

"She likes parties."

"She would have enjoyed the reception, yes."

"And the photographers."

"The camera loves her."

"What did your father do to convince you to take your sister's place?"

Her brow creased. "Excuse me?"

"Did he threaten you? Or was there a bribe involved? How did he get you to walk down the aisle and go through this whole…charade?"

"It's not a charade. I married you." She paused, gathering herself. "Of my own volition."

"So you volunteered?"

"No. I didn't volunteer. This isn't exactly a volunteer position."

He made a rough sound in the back of his throat and Kassiani calmly added, "But when my father presented me the…situation… I agreed that it was a problem and my family was indebted to you. It wouldn't be right for the Dukases to humiliate you. So I agreed to take Elexis's place so that the merger of businesses and families could still take place."

"Wasn't there a saint named Kassiani?"

"She was a hymnographer, not a virgin bride."

He gave her another long look. "I'm to be grateful the Dukas virgin has been forced onto me?"

She winced but refused to dwell on his sarcasm. "You're not being forced into anything. You can annul this afternoon's ceremony. Tomorrow. The next day. The day after." Her chin lifted. "As long as we don't consummate the marriage, you're free to annul this marriage at any time."

"Is that what you're hoping I'll do?"

"No. I said vows today and I intend to keep them. It is my expectation that we'll consummate the marriage tonight."

"And if I don't feel like falling into bed with…you?"

A lump filled her throat. She was aware of how disappointing she was as a woman. She could never compare, or compete, with Elexis. But she was still a woman and she had feelings. And hopes. And dreams. "I will do my best to make you want me."

The glance he shot her seemed laced with scorn and then he walked away from her, crossing the room to stand at the window, which faced the sea and the ancient Temple of Poseidon, which glowed golden in the setting sun. Tonight promised to be yet another spectacular sunset. Sunsets on Cape Sounio were the stuff of legends.

"Perhaps we should just dispense with this farce now," Damen said, his back still to her, his gaze fixed on the sea.

"Perhaps," she agreed serenely, grateful he couldn't see her hard jaw and how hurt and frustration welled. "I won't call you a coward if you do."

He turned suddenly, facing her. Temper blazed in his eyes. "I have done my part," he gritted. "I invested in Dukas Shipping. I sorted out your father's legal entanglements. I put aside my mistresses and waited patiently, celibately for your sister—"

"That was obviously a mistake."

"You're not helping your case, kitten."

"I don't think anything can. Because surely you don't want my sympathy, do you?" He didn't answer and her firm chin rose higher. "Maybe you should've spent more time with your future bride to make sure she was the right bride."

"Your father assured me Elexis was the right bride."

"And there is the root of all our problems. You trusted my father." Her full lips curved, but the smile didn't reach her eyes. "The world thinks you're smarter than that."

He stiffened, his eyes narrowing. "That does not sound very complimentary for a daughter to say of the father."

"Or for a bride to say of her new husband—"

"I wasn't going to say it."

She shrugged, and plucked at yet another pearl on her gown. "I'm a realist, I always have been." Kassiani drew a breath before continuing, her words cool and measured. "And I know who my family are. I know their strengths. I know their weaknesses." Her eyebrows flattened, her expression turning pensive. "Personally, I would not have gone into business with them. And I certainly wouldn't have climbed into bed with them. But you wanted the West Coast of North America. You wanted the ships and the ports and the agreements, and now you have them."

He walked back toward her, closing the distance with quiet, measured strides. Kassiani tried not to shrink as he stood directly before her, so tall that she had to tip her head back to see his face.

"You do not think highly of me," he said quietly.

Her heart did a painful double beat even as something like desire curled in her belly. The butterflies were back, but they weren't from fear. "I think you have underestimated the Dukas family."

"You didn't answer my question."

She hesitated for a long moment before looking up into his eyes. "I wouldn't marry a man I didn't hold in high esteem."

He stared down at her for even longer. "I'm not much for parties, either. We'll skip the reception and leave now."

CHAPTER TWO

DAMEN LED HER down stairs at the back of the villa, the hidden nature of the staircase indicating they were for the staff, before exiting the villa through a plain door, arriving into the villa's kitchen garden. They passed through herbs and fruit trees, and then turned left at an impressive beehive where they headed away from the orchard to a narrow path leading toward the water.

The path led to steep narrow stairs, and once down the wooden staircase they reached a simple dock, where a speedboat waited.

The driver of the boat offered her a hand in order to assist her into the boat, but Damen swept her into his arms and lifted her over the side, placing her inside on her feet.

She swayed in her heels, and immediately found the nearest seat.

Damen sat down opposite her and they were off, slowly at first and then picking up speed as they put distance between them and land.

The wind grabbed at her veil and Kassiani gripped the edge of her seat with one hand and tried to control her heavy veil with the other. From the water she could see the estate and villa. The estate was large, and one of the oldest on this part of the Athenian coast. The villa had been built facing the water, ensuring every room a sweeping view of the turquoise sea and the Temple of Poseidon on the hill across the water.

From their vantage point in the water, the garden glowed

with soft golden white light, with fairy lights strung in trees, and candelabras glimmering on the two dozen tables, while chandeliers inside the house emphasized the high ceilings and striking architecture. From here, the wedding reception looked downright magical, and Kassiani felt a pang of regret—this wasn't the wedding the guests had come for.

She tried to imagine their reaction when they discovered that the bride and groom were gone. She wondered how the evening would even go. Would anyone stay for the dinner once they realized there was no bride and groom? Or would others linger and dine and drink and take advantage of the splendid setting? She couldn't help thinking that there would be some who were grateful there would be no toasts, no speeches, no protracted dinner courses. And she was certain there were others, those who truly loved Damen, who would be confused, and worried.

The wedding really turned out to be a shambles.

What had Damen called it? A farce? A charade?

She felt a twinge of guilt followed by fresh anxiety. This was all so crazy, she hadn't really wrapped her head around anything that had taken place today. And now they were jetting off, but she had no idea where they were going. But as the cape fell farther behind, the boat suddenly slowed, drawing close to an enormous yacht in the bay, and then the engine turned off as they reached the yacht ladder at the back. Crew stood on a small platform awaiting them.

"Let's get your shoes off," Damen said. "I'd rather you not try to climb the stairs in those ridiculous shoes. How high are those heels anyway?"

"Too high," she admitted, grateful to remove the shoes that had pinched her feet all afternoon.

Once they were off, Damen swung Kassiani into his

arms and lifted her out, placing her on the platform. "Can you manage the stairs in that dress?" he asked.

"What are my options? Removing the dress here?" she answered.

He growled. *"No."*

She almost laughed. "Then yes, I can manage the stairs in this dress."

Her father's yacht had been built for her mother. And her father had never understood her mother's taste, and so the yacht had been over-the-top feminine with cream walls and gilded surfaces, floral tapestries and upholstery with horrendous columns everywhere to make the interior look like a Greek temple. Kassiani had found the superyacht garish and unappealing and she'd hated the few times her parents—she never knew which—decided they must all do a Mediterranean cruise together, trapping them on the yacht. She'd hated yachts and boats ever since, and held her breath as she was led up and down staircases and then down a narrow paneled hall toward bedrooms.

She wasn't sure if she was being taken to a master bedroom or just any bedroom, but when the uniformed staff opened a door and stepped back for her to enter, she was fairly certain it was the master bedroom by the fact that half the room was all floor-to-ceiling walls and glass doors with a private deck and a jaw-dropping view of the Temple of Poseidon, which had now been lit for the night and the dozens of majestic columns glowed yellow. The ancient ruins were beyond beautiful and she was drawn to the view, opening one set of the French doors to step out onto the deck.

And then on the opposite side of the bay, a villa and its grand gardens glimmered with light, competing for attention. Damen's villa.

For the first time since arriving in Greece, she felt the pull of Greece. Or maybe it was the stirring of her own Greek blood, recognizing that she'd come home. Her chest suddenly ached and she put a hand to her breast, pressing against the pain, overwhelmed by emotion.

What had she done?

"Second thoughts?" Damen's deep voice sounded behind her.

She turned suddenly, and struggled to smile but failed. "I don't know that I'd call them second thoughts, but certainly, this view gives me pause." Her head tipped as she studied him. "And you? Buyer's remorse?"

"You're a woman, not livestock. I haven't bought you."

"But I'm not the woman you wanted."

He didn't even hesitate. "No."

"I don't blame you for being disappointed. Elexis is stunning."

"She looks like your mother."

Kassiani stifled the pain. "And I take after Dad." She was grateful her voice sounded light, and breezy. She'd never want him to know how much it hurt being the Dukas her father called "pitiful."

"I didn't choose Elexis for her beauty."

Kassiani smiled politely. She didn't believe him for a moment. "Either way, I suppose it's a moot point now, isn't it?"

He looked from her to the Cape of Sounio, glowing gold with its famous marble temple built in 440 BC. It was remarkable that so much of the ancient temple remained.

"Did she ever intend to marry me?" he asked quietly.

Yes. No. Kass drew a deep breath. "I don't know," she answered honestly. "Elexis is a bit of an enigma."

"So there is more than what the eye sees?"

"No. The enigma is that she is just what you see. Beautiful."

His gaze narrowed and then he gave a half shrug. "It's been hours since breakfast. You must be starving—"

"Do I look as if I'm starving?" she interrupted with a faint smile.

He gave her another assessing glance. "I'll have a tray sent to you."

"Are you not eating?"

"I have things to take care of."

He didn't want to dine with her. Even though it was their wedding night. It shouldn't bother her. She shouldn't be attached to the outcome. She was here, the substitute bride, out of obligation, not affection. He was the humiliated groom. She shouldn't be surprised that he wanted to keep his distance. "A tray would be lovely." She nodded toward the glowing point. "Could I eat out here?"

"I'll have my steward set up a table."

She started to thank him but he was already walking out, and she watched him go, a lump filling her throat. This was not going to be easy.

Damen's office on the second deck was similar to his bedroom—a wall of windows, another wall of bookshelves and then large art pieces here and there. His oversize desk faced out, because he always preferred working with a view of the water. His parents might have preferred the land, and the olive groves they considered home, but he needed the sea. He craved the sea. It was when he faced out, toward the horizon of blue sky and blue sea, he could relax and breathe.

He ate only a few bites of his dinner before pushing it aside to concentrate on the agreements he'd pulled up on his laptop.

Agreements and contracts dating back three years, even though the discussion regarding merging Dukas and Alexopoulos began five years ago when Elexis was just graduating from college. Kristopher had been the one to approach Damen, suggesting that while each family was successful, they'd be even more powerful together, marrying the two families, and merging the two shipping empires, creating a truly remarkable empire. They'd be a world power together, controlling shipping lanes across the globe.

Damen had been intrigued but not sufficiently tempted because he knew Dukas's reputation. Dukas's deals could be shady as he tended to play a little too fast and loose. Damen might be ruthless, but he also knew that one's word mattered and he ran his business with integrity.

But two years later when Damen heard that Kristopher was dangling his daughter again, trying to find another Greek shipping company as a potential partner, he acted, flying out to San Francisco to discuss mutually beneficial scenarios. All of which included marriage to Dukas's daughter Elexis.

Damen wasn't emotionally attached to Elexis. She was simply a means to an end. And yet when he finally met Elexis, and saw how people responded to her, he was reassured, realizing she wouldn't just be a wife and mother to his heirs, but a valuable asset. The fact that people were drawn to her would be useful when entertaining clients. She could concentrate on the social niceties, leaving him free to focus on business.

Love never entered the equation because Damen didn't love people. He needed certain people in his life to get things done. He respected some of those he worked with, but tended to ignore most, having very little tolerance for people's weaknesses and idiosyncrasies. The more someone could prove beneficial, the more value he placed on them. It was cold, and unfeeling, but that was who he was and he wouldn't ever apologize for being pragmatic and strategic.

It was what had taken him from the olive groves on

Chios, to the helm of Aegean Shipping, which he renamed Alexopoulos Shipping of the Aegean after the elder Mr. Koumantaras died. The Koumantaras family wasn't happy that Mr. Koumantaras Sr. had left control of his business to the outsider, upstart Damen Alexopoulos, but Damen felt no remorse. Koumantaras's children had no desire to work for the family business. All they wanted was to live off the profits. So why should they care if the company changed its name?

One day Dukas Shipping would go the way of Aegean Shipping—the name would drop and the company itself would fold into the more powerful Alexopoulos Shipping.

Damen closed his laptop to look out the window at the now dark sky. At midnight the lights on the Temple of Poseidon would go out, but as it was only ten, the temple still glowed from the spotlights.

Damen tapped a finger on the arm of his chair, trying to ease the tension bottled within him. He hated how Kristopher Dukas had played him. He hated the feelings flooding him. He didn't like it when his temper flared. He had a hot temper. He used to have a horrendous temper. It had taken years to learn how to manage his anger, but today was testing him. Today made him want to let loose, and level something.

He thought of Kassiani in the master bedroom and closed his eyes and shook his head.

He didn't know why he'd allowed the steward to take her there. Kassiani should have been taken to a guest room. Somewhere out of his way. Somewhere he could forget her.

Instead she was in his room, waiting for his return.

His gut cramped.

He didn't want her. He didn't want to hurt her feelings, but he didn't want her. She wasn't the bride he'd been promised. Kristopher had promised the best daughter, and

Damen had believed him, investing heavily in Dukas Shipping's West Coast ports, building them up, buying new ships, aware that the heavy cash investment now would stabilize both of their businesses in the future. But the deal was off.

The marriage would be annulled.

And the contracts would soon be voided.

He'd already emailed his attorney to start the process of dissolution. Now it was just a matter of returning the Dukas girl to her father and moving forward the necessary legal action.

Her meal finished, Kassiani left the table and retreated inside to study the luxurious master bedroom. At least, she assumed it was the master bedroom, which meant Damen would be returning at some point, and they would be alone. Here. In the bedroom.

She, who had only pecked Damen on the lips at the chapel, needed to find the confidence to sleep with him. Correction, *not sleep*, but have sex with him, because if the marriage wasn't fully consummated, Damen could annul it and then the Dukases would lose everything.

Kassiani might not be the favored daughter, but she was loyal to her family and protective of the company. She'd agreed to marry Damen so that Dukas Shipping wouldn't be destroyed by legal actions. Damen could destroy them. His demands for restitution would bankrupt the company.

As her father baldly put it this morning—he couldn't afford to pay Damen back. The wedding had to happen, and the marriage consummated.

Which meant Kassiani had to seduce Damen tonight. It wouldn't be easy. She wasn't just a virgin, but a virgin with zero experience. Before the peck in the chapel, she'd only ever been kissed once before, a bumbling fumbling kiss that had been so wet and distasteful that she'd never wanted to kiss again.

Compared to that wet, violent assault on her mouth, today's chapel kiss had been rather exhilarating. When he'd tilted her chin up to kiss her, she'd felt a little shiver of anticipation, and he'd smelled lovely as his head dropped, his mouth brushing hers. His lips had felt firm and cool, and yet they'd somehow made her feel warm, and tingly. Her lips continued to tingle even after he'd lifted his head. She'd found herself wishing the kiss had lasted longer. She was curious as to what more would feel like, and with a longer kiss, perhaps she could process her thoughts and all the different sensations. Kass liked data and analysis. Information was immensely helpful.

More information was needed now.

How was she to seduce Damen when she had no knowledge of such things? Of course she knew what men's bodies looked like. She didn't live in the Dark Ages. She had a brother. She had a father. The internet was full of photographs, and movies, and she'd just have to piece together from movies what men would like.

From what she recalled, men seemed to like stripteases. They liked lap dances. They liked titillation, including women on their knees, obedient and eager to please.

Kassiani tried to imagine kneeling before Damen, her hands on his thighs, fingers moving toward the zipper of his trousers.

The image made her feel peculiar. Heat washed through her, making her skin prickle, and her breasts peak. The hot ball of tension seemed to center low in her belly, pulsing a little between her thighs. She was nervous and excited at the same time. Her entire world had been turned upside down. She'd come to Athens five days ago expecting to attend her sister's wedding. Instead she'd been woken by her father early this morning with the news that he expected her to marry Elexis's groom. And Kassiani, so desperate to earn her father's favor, had. Now instead of returning to San Francisco, she was to remain in Greece, and make a new life for herself as Damen's wife.

Kassiani shot a glance into the wood-framed mirror on the wall. She was still wearing Elexis's wedding dress, and the lace panels that had been added were pulling at the seams. Even in a corset, even with the additional panels added to the dress, the gown was too tight. The fabric pulled in all the wrong places.

Kass had never let herself dream about her wedding day, but if she was being honest, she'd say it certainly wasn't the wedding that took place today, and she certainly wouldn't have chosen this dress…a dress that made her look even curvier and stockier with all the lace panels.

No, she would have chosen something simple—an off-the-shoulder white satin gown that minimized her bust and skimmed her hips, before falling into a long graceful skirt in the same clean white satin. There would have been no plunging necklines and no bustle and no ornate beading adding thickness and weight to the lace panels worked into the bodice and skirt.

Kassiani placed a hand to the plunging neckline, running her fingertips lightly over her curves. Her breasts were beyond voluptuous. She'd always hated the thickness of her hips and thighs, as well as the shape of her belly, somewhat round as if she practiced belly dancing regularly, instead of the hours she spent on a treadmill walking, walking, walking, forever trying to reduce her form, wanting to be lean like her mother and sister. She would never be lean.

Her exterior was what it was—it couldn't be changed—and she was certain her new husband was disappointed, which was why she had to prove herself. She had to prove to him tonight that she fully intended to be a good wife. She'd find a way to satisfy him.

But how?

And what if she couldn't get him to respond?

Kass grabbed her phone and, while struggling out of her gown and layers of girdles and undergarments, researched men and arousal. Peeling her stockings off, she found quite a few sites offering numerous tips on how to please your man in bed, ranging from "Twelve Erogenous Zones That Shouldn't Be Ignored" to a very useful and practical article on "How to Give Unforgettable Oral Sex."

Naked, she headed into the adjoining white marble bathroom and, careful not to get her hair wet—it was still coiled up in an elaborate updo—she used the body wash in the shower to try to rub some of the marks out of her skin, but the angry red marks created by the corset weren't ready to fade. Leaving the shower, she wrapped herself in the white robe hanging on the back of the door, and then sat down on the edge of the bathtub and began reading everything she could about pleasing a man.

She was still reading when she heard a firm knock on the bathroom door. "Are you hiding, *mikrí sou gynaíka*?"

Her Greek was a little rusty, but not so rusty she didn't understand his words. *Are you hiding, my little wife?*

She jumped up and turned her phone off. "No." Kassiani opened the door and faced him, tugging the lapels of the robe so that they better covered her chest. "I'm using your robe. I hope that is okay. I'm sorry. I didn't think to bring any clothes with me."

"I don't think either of us was thinking clearly." He hesitated, and then shrugged. "This isn't going to work. I'll ask the crew to find something for you to wear and then my security will get you back to the villa at Sounio."

"Am I that much of a disappointment?"

"You're not a disappointment."

"Then why send me away without giving me a chance?"

"Because I was engaged to Elexis, not you."

"But Elexis left and I was there."

"The Dukas sisters are not interchangeable!"

"Because I'm not beautiful like her?"

"Because you're not hard like her." He didn't quite yell, but he flung the words at her with enough ferocity to make her flinch. He must have seen her reaction because he dropped his voice. "I wanted a wife who wouldn't feel. A woman I couldn't bruise. I don't know you very well, Petra Kassiani, but my gut says you feel, and feel deeply."

Heat rushed through her, and shame, because he was right. She did feel deeply but she hated that aspect of her personality, far preferring her intellect over her emotions. "I understand the kind of marriage you want. I won't ask you to romance me. I won't expect flowers and poetry—"

"Or tenderness? Or kindness? Or patience?"

"I can't believe you're capable of all of the above."

"Well, I am. Trust me."

"You were marrying Elexis to help save Dukas Shipping."

"I was marrying Elexis to dismantle Dukas Shipping."

Her eyes widened and her heart skipped a beat. "I don't believe you," she whispered.

"If you stay here, if you remain my wife and the agreements and contracts hold, there will be no Dukas Shipping in five years. It will all be Alexopoulos Shipping of the Aegean."

She stared at him, skeptical, but also wary. "Is this your way of making me throw up my arms and run back to my father? Am I to choose him and his business over you?"

"I am nothing to you. You are nothing to me—"

"I married you. You are my husband."

"But you do not know me. You should have no loyalty to me."

"I pledged to care for you and be a good wife. I intend to keep my vow."

"Even though I want to destroy what's left of your father's business?"

She didn't immediately answer, taking needed time to form an answer. "From the beginning this was to be a merger of families and businesses. The stronger business always wins in mergers. You are the stronger partner and change was inevitable."

He turned away and walked through the French doors to the deck. She could see him run his hand across his jaw, once, and then again. He was battling himself, she thought. He was battling and she didn't even know his fight, but whatever it was, she was firmly on his side. She had to be. She had chosen him, and she'd wanted a new life. A different life. She'd wanted to be an Alexopoulos, and not a Dukas, and if she wasn't careful he'd cart her back to the mainland and she'd be back with her father, which was the last place she wanted to be.

Kassiani followed him outside. Clouds half covered the moon, casting shadows on the deck. She couldn't see Damen's face clearly. But his shoulders were rigid, and even from this angle, he looked utterly unapproachable.

"Damen."

"Go back inside. I can't think clearly with you near me."

"Maybe that's good."

"It's not."

The night had cooled and a wind blew, tugging at her hair, and the label of her thick white robe. "Please, just give me a chance—"

"For God's sake, do not beg, Kassiani."

"Just give me a chance. *One* chance. That's all I ask."

"Why?"

"I want out. I want a life away from my family—"

"You're not going to get a happy family with me."

"I'm not asking for a fairy tale. I'm not pretty and popular. I find dating a nightmare. I'm so awkward but at the same time, I'm practical. I know you were marrying my sister because you wanted heirs. Obviously she's not ready to marry and be a mother, but I am. I want children. I'll be a good mother, too. So give me a chance to show you I could be a good wife, and…please…you. If I can't, and you have no…interest…despite my best efforts, then I will go home, and I'll accept your decision. But I can't accept rejection before I've had a chance to prove myself—"

"This isn't about you," he gritted, spinning around, features twisted. "This is about your father manipulating me—"

"But you got everything you wanted…the deals, the ports, the ships, the agreements, everything but Elexis. And you said you didn't love her, so why can't I be a substitute bride? Why can't I be the woman to give you your children? Is it because I'm so much plainer?"

"No."

"You protested too quickly." She struggled to smile. "I don't believe you. But that's okay. I know what I look like—"

"Stop it, Kass!" He grabbed her by the upper arms and gave her a shake. "Stop this madness. Because it is madness. I may not have been born with much, but I would never take a woman against her will, and you were forced into this marriage by your father to save his hide, not yours."

"But that's not true. This marriage saves mine. This marriage gets me out." Her voice broke. Tears fell. "I hated living in that house on Nob Hill. I have never fit in, never belonged, and I'm fully aware of who I am in that family. I'm the ugly one. The embarrassing one. The one they choose to leave behind. Marrying you lets me escape that legacy. You give me a new life, and a future."

"You'll be no happier with me."

She hesitated, a lump welling in her throat, a lump so big it made swallowing hurt. "I know it's not easy to look at me—"

"Good God!" He gave her another shake. "Do not say such things. You are not your sister, but you are not ugly, not even remotely ugly." His grip eased, his hands half sliding down her arms. "Don't ever say such a thing again because it's a lie and you seem far too intelligent to believe lies and mistruths."

Her head jerked up and she searched his face. "Could you make love to me?"

"Kassiani."

"You can't imagine it?"

"That's not the point."

"But it is. If I can please you, and prove to you I'm a good wife, you might realize this is the right marriage." Her chin lifted, her expression provocative, despite the trace of tears. "So do we have a deal, Damen Alexopoulos? I know you like making deals, so make one with me."

"This is a terrible deal."

"Because if you lose, you're stuck with me?"

"No, because if you lose, you'll apparently be weeping all over my villa and I'll feel like a—oh, what is the word in English? A *beast*? An *ogre*?"

"A schmuck."

"A schmuck," he echoed.

"But I won't be weeping and you won't have to feel like a schmuck if you give me a fair chance. I understand your objections. I know you don't want me. I know you have no feelings for me. But history is filled with arranged marriages and many of them turned out to be good partnerships. Beneficial relationships. Why can't we be one of those?"

"So how do we know who wins?"

"You give me to dawn. If we consummate our marriage tonight, I win. If we don't, you win, and you can have your security return me to the villa first thing in the morning."

He sighed and dragged a hand through his thick dark hair, rifling it on end. "Do you have a plan, kitten?"

"I do. I'm going to seduce you."

CHAPTER THREE

HE HADN'T COME to the bedroom to make love to his new wife. He'd come to send her home, and yet she was fierce and stubborn, determined to fight for this marriage.

So different from Elexis, who hadn't even bothered to show up for the ceremony. So different from Elexis, who couldn't even hold a conversation with him. Kassiani could hold a conversation and more. She was fierce, smart, *eloquent*. She would have been an incredible trial attorney. She'd be amazing in the boardroom.

Maybe that's why he was here, sitting in one of the leather chairs in the master bedroom, telling Kassiani to unpin her hair and then shake it out, before letting her try to entertain him.

He was intrigued by her, curious as to her next move.

Her next move proved to be a rather awkward, but earnest, dance in front of him.

She was still wearing his robe but every now and then a lapel slipped open, revealing the pale slope of a full breast, or a knee and thigh.

He hadn't allowed himself to think of her as a woman before this, because she hadn't been his woman, but as she danced, her hips slowly, sensually gyrating, her arms lifted over her head, eyes half-closed as she swayed, he couldn't look away. He was fairly certain she'd never done this before, which was maybe what made her efforts so appealing. He hadn't thought he'd find her arousing, and yet he was hard, and growing harder as she danced and swayed, using her body to entice him.

He watched her from beneath heavy lids, body heating, blood humming in his veins. He'd wanted to be done with her. He'd come to his room to dispense with her, and yet here she was, dancing as if her life depended on it. As though he were a sultan, and she a disgraced member of his harem.

And perverse as the thought was, that, too, aroused him. The only way he felt anything, anymore, was through sex. Hard, carnal sex. Sex threaded with power. Sex laced with pain. He hadn't always been this way. He'd been…normal… once.

He'd had feelings, and tenderness. But that had been stripped from him in his teenage years, along with his pride, leaving only failure and shame.

It's why he wanted to marry Elexis. She was hard. He wouldn't break her. But Kassiani…she was entirely something else.

And she was entirely something else right now, as she slowly sank down, going to her knees before him. Her hands rested lightly on his knees and her head tipped back to look up into his face.

He didn't know what he saw in his face, but whatever she did see, it emboldened her. She ran her hands lightly up his quadriceps, her palms warm against his thighs. Reaching his hips, she lightly stroked down, brushing the inside of his thighs. His shaft throbbed. He felt as if he would burst out of his skin in a moment. His virginal little bride was not acting so very virginal in that moment.

It had been a long time since he'd been so turned on. A long time since his chest felt heat and warmth along with his groin. Normally only his erection worked, but tonight his entire body heated and thrummed as her hands stroked back up his thighs, moving toward his zipper.

Damen had to steel himself to keep from making a sound.

He watched, fascinated, as she unzipped him and reached into his cotton briefs to draw him out. He was long and thick and he pulsed in her soft, warm hand.

He wanted to tell her to wrap her fingers around him. He wanted to tell her how to stroke him—firmly, from the base of his shaft to the tip of his rounded head. He wanted what he wanted, and yet, he was also curious to see what she'd do next, and how she intended to satisfy him.

Her fingers slowly curved around him and she lowered her head to touch the tip of her tongue to the head of his shaft.

He stifled his growl of appreciation as her tongue lapped at him, licking the throbbing tip as if he were a lollipop or ice-cream cone.

It was all he could do not to rock his hips. He wanted to be in her mouth. He wanted the pressure of her hand and the wet heat of her mouth, and she wasn't quite getting the hang of it yet, but just watching her lick him, and suck him, made him hungrier, and fiercer.

She was trying so hard to please him, and she was applying herself so passionately to the task, that every flick of her tongue across his swollen head made him groan inwardly. She was either a splendid actress, or she genuinely enjoyed sucking him. The fact that she might just enjoy this…night…had never once crossed his mind. He hadn't ever thought of her wanting him, or desiring him, and watching her lavish him with attention made him want to explode.

He stopped there, aware that these weren't the thoughts of a considerate husband.

Not that he'd ever be a truly good, considerate husband, because he wasn't a good or considerate man. He was too bitter and broken. Too ambitious. Too driven. He'd come from nowhere, having risen up from nothing—literally olive trees and a stone hut in the middle of a hilltop or-chard—and then even that had been taken from him, taken by those who believed money made them better than others, that money gave them the right to use and abuse.

It's why he'd worked so hard his entire life—to distance himself from the victim he'd been.

Having hit the absolute bottom, he knew he'd never be weak again.

His world was strength, power, domination. It was his one and only goal.

He wanted a family to prove that he'd overcome a dark past, and he had the means to ensure they'd be safe. They'd be comfortable, guarded, protected. His children would be able to go to the best schools. They'd have the best secu-rity. They'd never be exploited. But he needed a wife who would love them, because he didn't love. He didn't have normal emotions and feelings, and there was no room for feelings, just as there would be no romance.

Should he take Kassiani to his bed, it would be strictly business. Just like consummating the marriage was serious business. The moment he took her virginity, there would be no going back. The moment he claimed her, there would be no annulment.

Did he *want* to claim her?

He studied her from beneath heavy lids, his erection aching in her hands, the thick tip damp from her mouth.

Even though she was the wrong bride, she was still a Dukas and the marriage still gave him what he wanted—all of North America's West Coast ports. All the Dukas ships. All the trade agreements.

Part of him wanted to punish the Dukas family for play-ing him, but that would be cutting off his nose to spite his face. Kassiani would meet his needs just as well as Elexis. Maybe even better because his children did need a mother who would feel and care and fight for them. They'd need one parent with a heart.

He should just take her to bed, and claim her. He wouldn't be rough with her, even though he liked hot, hard sex. Sex without apology. He'd never made love to a woman and felt love. Sex—intercourse—was a release, and it felt good after he climaxed, but there wasn't much else he felt in the bedroom, other than loathing. He'd never tell anyone but he could barely tolerate being touched. He could barely endure being inside his skin. It was always a fight, a battle, to not remember the past. To not let memories resurface.

It's why he'd kept mistresses over the years, not girlfriends. It's why he'd wanted an arranged marriage. It was clean, clear, undemanding. There would be no affection, no emotion, no demands.

He avoided drama at all costs. He avoided feelings, and he certainly avoided feeling anything that hurt. Damen couldn't even remember the last time he felt tenderness. And yet, glancing down to his lap where Kassiani's dark head bobbed over his thick shaft, he felt strangely undone. It crossed his mind that he didn't deserve her. It crossed his mind that she shouldn't have been the sacrificial lamb.

Elexis was so much better suited to him. Consummating the marriage with her would have been far easier because he could take her and leave her and there would be no guilt. No remorse.

Tonight, even if he managed not to physically hurt Kassiani by taking her virginity, he suspected she'd still be bruised by this new life. She'd be bruised by him. He knew she hadn't been treated well by her family, and now she'd married a man who wouldn't treat her much better. Worse, she'd be grateful for the crumbs thrown her way.

The thought made his skin crawl.

She deserved so much more. She might be a Dukas but she wasn't shallow and hollow like the rest of them—

Kassiani's head suddenly lifted and her eyes met his. Something in her expression made his body tighten all over again, his shaft pulsing against her full lips.

He couldn't tear his gaze away from his head pressed to her mouth. It was hot and dirty and sexy all at the same time.

He shouldn't have allowed his virginal bride to go down on her knees in his white robe with nothing else on. He shouldn't have let her take him in her sweet, hot mouth, not when he was still trying to decide if he wanted to keep her. He was an ass. Selfish, ruthless, uncaring.

And desperately aroused.

So unusual for him and his numb body.

"You don't have to do that," he rasped, involuntarily reaching out to run the pad of his thumb across the sweep of her cheekbone. Her skin was soft, and warm. He wondered if she was as warm between her thighs. He wondered if she was wet.

"Why not?" she answered unsteadily. "Am I doing it wrong?"

Her question, in her low, throaty voice, made his body shudder. It didn't help that she followed her question with a light lick up the side of his shaft. He felt her lick all the way to the base of his penis, his balls tightening with pleasure. "You are doing quite well," he gritted.

The corner of her lips turned up, her long black lashes lowering over eyes that seemed to gleam with satisfaction. He'd never seen anything so erotic, this curvaceous little siren, his unexpected, swapped bride.

"I want to make you come," she whispered, "but obviously I'm not doing something right because it hasn't happened."

"It hasn't *happened* because I'm holding myself back."

For a moment there was just silence as her eyes widened as she processed what he'd said.

And then she rose slightly on her knees, her face lifting, expression surprised. "You can do that?"

"I can do many things."

Her expression shifted, increasingly curious and mind-blowingly sensual, reminding him of a courtesan rather than an untutored virgin. "Show me," she said, her hands on his inner thighs, her fingertips against the base of his shaft.

He clamped his jaw tight, fighting to steady his breathing. He had no idea why she tested his control. At twenty-three she was thirteen years younger than he, but in that moment he felt as if she had all the power and experience. "Show you what, *gataki*?"

"How to do it. How to make you feel so good that you can't…hold back."

"I think you're doing fine for a beginner."

"*Fine* is my least favorite word in the English language. *Fine* indicates mediocrity. I hate mediocrity."

He found himself almost smiling and then he clasped her face and kissed her deeply, claiming her mouth the way he should have in the beginning. She froze and stiffened, and then after a moment her lips softened, parting for him.

It was in that moment he stopped vacillating.

It was in that moment when she opened her mouth, giving herself to him, that he knew he would take her, claim her and make her his.

There would be no turning back. Not now, not anymore.

He took her mouth the way he intended to take her—with single-minded focus, his tongue sweeping the seam of her lips before thrusting into the warmth of her mouth and finding the hollows of her cheeks, the inside of her lips, the pressure and release so similar to what his body would do to hers, and how he'd find a rhythm and make her feel.

She whimpered softly, her hands reaching up to cover his, her fingers wrapping around his wrists. But she wasn't pulling his hands away. No, she was pressing his hands against her jaw, pressing him to her for more sensation even as her fingertips stroked the inside of his wrists and the sensitive mound of his palms.

Blood roared through his ears, pulsing in his veins. He felt his shaft bob, thick and heavy with need.

Sweeping her into his arms, Damen carried Kassiani to the bed. She lay on her back, looking up at him, the white robe parting to reveal pale skin. Her curves were ripe, the fabric clinging to the blatant fullness of her breasts and swell of her tummy. He tugged on the sash of the robe, untying it before pushing the robe back, exposing her.

She was an hourglass—full breasts with dark pink nipples, narrow waist and generous hips perfect to cradle him. He'd expected her to have a patch of trimmed dark curls, but instead she was bare, and the sight of her so smooth tested his control.

He needed to take it slowly, though. She wasn't experienced. He didn't want to hurt her. It was important she was ready for him.

"Eísai axiagápitos," he murmured, telling her she was lovely, because she was. The dark pink of her nipples were in stark contrast to her alabaster skin, and the tight tips called to him, as did the bareness between her thighs.

He leaned over her to lightly trace one puckered areola with his tongue, before turning to the other. Each swirl of his tongue was awesome. He leaned over her, his mouth closing over one taut nipple and sucking it the way she'd sucked his cock.

She whimpered, one hand pressed to the mattress, fingers flexed as he worked the sensitive peak. He cupped her other breast as he teased and nipped at her nipple, enjoying her soft, hoarse cries of pleasure. Her skin was warm and satiny smooth as he pressed a kiss between her breasts, and then lower to her trembling belly.

Every kiss he placed was rewarded with another throaty pant of pleasure. He continued kissing lower, even as he caressed up, shaping her, discovering how very sensitive she was.

He pressed one of her knees down, creating space for him, and he found himself just wanting to look at her, and drink in her feminine shape—soft curves and secret shadows. His shaft ached.

Damen dipped his head, his lips brushing the inside of her creamy thigh. She sighed at the feel of his lips. She sighed and stirred restlessly as he continued kissing his way up the inside of her thigh, his tongue drawing lazy circles on the tender skin where her thigh joined her hip.

Her skin burned and she smelled sweet, like honey in the sun. He wanted to drink her, but he was determined to make her wait, wanting her fully aroused, and wet, before he entered her.

She squirmed and exhaled hard as he placed a kiss at the top of her mound, just above her lips.

She exhaled again, another devastatingly sexy gasp of pleasure and wonder, as he breathed on her, letting his breath warm her, and tease her.

"You are bare," he said, stroking her mound with a fingertip, lightly caressing the plump outer lip that was perfectly smooth. "You've been waxed."

She shuddered and closed her eyes. "I was told you would prefer me this way."

"Who told you?"

She shook her head, her teeth catching on her lower lip.

He continued stroking her, lightly down the one side and then up over the other until he reached the top again.

Her thighs were trembling. Her body quivered and she was breathing more quickly, her breasts rising and falling, her nipples even tighter than they'd been a moment ago.

"Have you ever been waxed before?" he asked, his tongue dipping between those plump bare lips to flick across her.

She jumped at the touch, reaching for him with one hand, her fingers brushing his shoulder before tangling in his hair.

"Hmm?" he persisted, tongue tracing her folds, discovering she wasn't just damp, but wet. Soaked. Her hips rotated beneath him and he licked the silken inner lips, tasting her. She tasted like sun-kissed honey, too, hot and sweet.

"Never waxed before," she panted, as he used two fingers to trace her, and shape her, her outer lips, then her inner lips, skirting her damp core.

"Do you like it like this?" he asked, his mouth following his fingers, teasing, tasting, turning her into a mass of quivering nerve endings. "So smooth and bare?"

"It's different—" And she broke off in a gasp as he drew her clit into his mouth, sucking on the nub, even as he slipped his fingers inside her, stroking her on the inside.

Her hips rose and fell as he played her, and when she cried out as she climaxed, he gave her a moment to settle before spreading her knees and sinking into her, claiming her as his, forevermore.

It was more than a pinch when he thrust into her. It hurt, and part of her objected to the intense fullness and pressure, but then as the sting eased and her body relaxed, the sense of fullness gave way to new and interesting sensations, with the uppermost sensation being that of wonder.

She loved the feeling of him on her. She loved the slow hard strokes of him in her. Her lips parted as she struggled to catch her breath, but it was virtually impossible to contain the tension and pleasure.

She positively buzzed from head to toe. Closing her eyes, she gave herself over to feelings, and they were such good feelings. She could still remember how his mouth had felt on her. It was unlike anything she'd ever felt before. His mouth and tongue and breath had created so many different impressions—each of them thrilling and arousing.

Tonight had to be the most incredible night of her life.

She knew she'd never forget it. How could she when Damen was making her body hum and sing, lighting her up as if she was a living Christmas tree? Each of his deep thrusts hit a sensitive spot inside her, and as he moved faster, and harder, she arched to receive him, glowing, burning, feeling incredibly alive.

She was going to come again, she thought, as the sensation continued to build and center, intensifying, the pleasure so intense it was almost painful, and just when she thought she couldn't hold on to the exquisite sensations a moment longer, she shattered all over again, her body climaxing, rippling with one delicious wave of bliss after another.

Two orgasms on her wedding night. Amazing.

And then he groaned and stiffened, plunging deep within her, and she realized he'd just climaxed, too.

After a bit he shifted his weight, stretching out next to her, leaving his arm around her waist, holding her to his side.

Peace flooded her. She hadn't been sure about tonight,

but everything was beautiful, and for once in her life, she felt perfect.

Kassiani tried to keep her eyes open but she was exhausted, and she fell asleep nestled to Damen's chest, her legs tangled with his.

Later in the night, Kass felt the bed shift. Damen was moving away, rolling toward the edge. The mattress dipped and then he eased himself out of the bed.

She didn't know why she feigned sleep and yet she listened to the bedroom door open and close.

It was only when the door clicked shut that she opened her eyes. Moonlight spilled into the room. The Sounio Cape was almost dark, everyone in bed for the night.

Kassiani didn't know if Damen was permanently gone or if he'd be coming back. She didn't know where he'd gone, or why.

Sleepily, she struggled to sort through her feelings. So much had happened in one day. Her father's announcement that she needed to take Elexis's place. Her shock and initial resistance until she realized that marrying Damen would be good for her. It'd give her opportunities she'd never have trapped in the Dukas mansion on Nob Hill.

And once she said yes to her father's idea, the wedding gown alteration and the rigorous wedding prep—the salt scrub, the waxing, the hair mask, the application of lotions and polish—before the wedding itself.

Damen's fury as he discovered the truth about his bride.

The reception they didn't attend.

The early departure in the speedboat.

The arrival on the yacht.

And then Damen, finally claiming her.

Her body was sore, but not unbearably so. She also felt warm and languid in a way she never felt before. Their coming together was nothing like she had imagined it would be. It wasn't sex but something bigger, something more, something…significant.

And she couldn't explain how or why, but she sensed that Damen felt it, too.

CHAPTER FOUR

DAMEN LEFT THE mahogany-paneled bedroom to tackle the details needing attention, details like sending staff to retrieve Kassiani's belongings from his villa, and changing the travel plan because he couldn't stomach the idea of taking Kassiani on the same honeymoon that had been planned for Elexis. Elexis needed people and activity and so they were to spend a few days anchored off the island of Mykonos so Elexis could have her fill of the cafés and restaurants, nightclubs and high-end shops, before continuing to Santorini for more of the same.

Damen didn't know his new wife well yet, but he could safely say that Kassiani would prefer not to shop and cared little about hip nightclubs and trendy bars.

While staff went to collect Kassiani's luggage, he discussed the change in itinerary with his captain, and then retreated to the far end of the top deck so he could be alone, needing the night air to clear his head and cool his body.

It was rather shocking to discover that his body still hummed with desire and hunger. Usually after sex he was done. Sated. After a long night of sexual play, he wanted nothing more to do with his mistress for a length of time, but right now he still craved his shy, innocent bride who seemed to be anything but shy in bed.

He shouldn't want Kassiani this much. He shouldn't already want to return to her. And yet right now all he wanted was to be with her again, to push her back onto the bed and feel her softness beneath him. He wanted her heat and shape, and he was impatient to discover all the mysteries she had yet to share.

Frustrated, Damen left the deck, retreating to a guest bedroom on a different level from the master, stripping off his clothes to take a cold shower before stretching out on the bed.

He refused to think about her anymore tonight. This wasn't normal. He didn't like feeling his control slip. She was just a small part of his world, and he needed to remember that.

Sometime before dawn they pulled anchor and set off. It was still dark out when Kassiani woke to the hum of the engine, and opening her eyes, she glanced over to the space next to her and discovered it was empty. She reached out and touched the place Damen had been earlier and his spot was cool.

Had Damen never come back?

She looked past his side of the bed to the tall windows with their view of the deck and sea. The sky was still purple, and stars glittered overhead, and yet they were no longer anchored in the bay, but powering through the Greek islands.

Kassiani reached for her phone to check the time but she hadn't brought a charger and it had died during the night.

For several minutes she lay there, thinking of Damen, and what had happened between them, and she wondered if she should go find him, but knew it would look silly to search for him on his own ship.

And then she felt the yacht surge forward, and realized that the engines had started because they were leaving the bay. She lay on the bed and gave herself over to the lovely motion of the yacht traveling through the water. The gentle rocking motion lulled her back to sleep.

When she woke again, it was morning, the sun high in the sky, and a breakfast tray waited for her on the table next to the bed, with a pale pink robe draped across the foot of the bed and her set of luggage from the villa standing sentry next to the door.

Kassiani slid from the bed and picked up the robe, slipping her arms into the silk sleeves. The robe was soft and incredibly light, hugging her curves as she tied the sash at her waist. Glancing into the mirror, she loved the color of the kimono. It was a pale pink that deepened to a rose at the thigh and by the hem had become a gorgeous burgundy. Burnt-orange peonies and delicate little birds had been hand-painted on the watercolor background and yet the cinched sash made her waist look wide and her body overly lush.

She really, truly hated her shape.

Damen hadn't seemed to mind when they were together, but then, he'd left in the night and hadn't returned. What did that mean?

She set the breakfast tray on the bed before climbing back in, and pulling the covers up. As she sat back down, she felt a little sore.

Suddenly she felt nervous and shy.

What did Damen think of last night? Was he disappointed? Or had she been able to satisfy him?

She reached for the pot of coffee, and filled a cup. Steam rose from her cup so it was still quite hot. The tray had only recently been delivered, then. She wondered if Damen had brought the tray to her and then grimaced. Unlikely.

She took a sip from her cup, savoring the coffee. She loved her coffee black, and strong, and this coffee was perfect. Everything was fine. Damen was fine. Last night had been fine…more than fine… There was no reason to worry. Things were just new and different.

She took deep calming breaths as she sipped her coffee, practicing the yoga breathing she'd learned, the breathing more helpful than the yoga poses that had just made her feel clumsy. Just like that, Kassiani felt a wave of insecurity, and she deliberately smashed her fears. Worrying wouldn't accomplish anything. Instead, she reached for one of the pastries, selecting a flaky *bougatsa* filled with custard, and tried to decide how she was going to spend her first day as Mrs. Damen Michael Alexopoulos.

Damen had more than enough work to do to spend the day, and evening, at his desk.

He told himself he didn't need to worry about his new bride, that it wasn't a good use of his time and energy to obsess about her.

They'd survived the wedding. They'd consummated the marriage. They would be together for the next week or so as they sailed the Aegean Sea. Why should he worry? Kassiani had an entire yacht of entertainment at her disposal. She'd be content, and for his part, he was far more content away from her. She wasn't what he'd expected. He hadn't been able to sleep even in the guest bedroom. His body didn't feel like his body. His senses remained stirred. Everything in him was still alert, aroused.

It boggled his mind that he'd responded to her the way he had. He didn't normally feel so much in bed. Sex was exercise, a release. It didn't move him. It didn't confound him. But Kassiani had made sex new somehow. New and fascinating and unbelievably good. Better than some of the best sex with his most experienced mistresses.

Great sex, hot sex, hard, carnal sex, wasn't normally an issue for him, but he had rules, and walls, and boundaries and hot, hard carnal sex stayed in the bedroom, and didn't intrude on the rest of his life, and yet last night, even after leaving the bedroom, he felt her.

He thought of her.

He wanted her.

Even now he wasn't relaxed. Instead, he'd wanted to return to the bedroom and wake her with his mouth and fingers and cock. He wanted to hear her make those whimpering sounds as she came. He wanted to feel her body arch, her full breasts crushed to his chest, her moisture creating the perfect silken slickness for each of his hard thrusts.

Damen jerked off twice in that damn guest bedroom, his mind and body too aroused and refusing to be soothed.

Feeling so much was disorienting, and distracting. He kept having washes of memory. Memory of home. Memory of olive groves. Memory of a lean tan boy who'd once loved deeply, before becoming a monster.

Damen slammed his hand against the door, slamming away memories, suppressing sensation and emotion. He refused to go there. He refused to get caught up in the past. And if Kassiani was wakening the past, then far better he take control of their relationship now before she let the monster loose.

In the end, it was a disappointing day for a newly married woman.

Kassiani had tried to keep busy. She'd tried to remain upbeat. She'd tried to fill her hours, which was why she swam in the fitness pool, sunbathed on the sundeck, napped for an hour in the shade, found two books in the library and watched a movie in the theater, with meals and snacks and cold beverages served in between by attentive staff.

Kassiani had successfully kept herself occupied, but as she finished her after-dinner liqueur, and changed for bed without a single appearance by her new husband, she couldn't help feeling let down. Maybe even betrayed.

Yes, it was a superyacht, but theoretically, it wasn't *that* big. He knew she was there. And he hadn't once sought her out.

Turning out the light, she sat on the foot of the bed in the dark. Her emotions swirled within her, cloudy and confusing. Last night when she had fallen asleep next to him, she felt safe. Secure. There had been no regrets, just relief and surprise…maybe even joy. The lovemaking *had* been a joy.

She hadn't expected that. She hadn't expected to feel so good in his arms. She hadn't expected to relish the sensation of him, in her, filling her.

But now, in the fading light of day, she didn't feel as calm and content. In fact, she didn't feel calm at all. She was unsettled, and bewildered.

The lovemaking had been so intimate. They'd explored each other's bodies and given each other so much pleasure, and yet now Damen had retreated, and she didn't know if it was intentional or not, but today he'd shut her out, completely.

She drew her knees up to her chest, and sighed, because on second thought, she was sure it was intentional.

Damen Alexopoulos was a man who left nothing to chance. If she hadn't seen him, it was because he'd avoided her today, not easy on a yacht because they were confined. At sea.

If he hadn't bothered to find her, and speak to her, and check on her well-being, then it was because he wanted her to understand that he was the boss. Not her. He was teaching her her place. And her place wasn't with him.

It was deflating, especially after what had taken place last night.

But in a strange way she understood. They had been so

intimate, and so open, that it was understandable that today he wanted to take back some of that power, because Greek men were all about power. Her father had been the same. Damen was letting her know that she might be his wife, but she wasn't an equal, and she most definitely wasn't his partner.

He wasn't going to go to her tonight. He would lay down the routine now, the pattern that they'd live by. The sooner she understood that he had control, and he valued control, the better.

But lying in the guest bedroom he'd taken since his room had become Kassiani's, he couldn't relax, instantly hard every time he thought of her. Last night she'd felt so good. Just remembering her soft skin and her soft pants and husky little breaths turned him on even now. He needed relief and he wanted to return to the master bedroom, and take her again, and he was certain she wouldn't refuse him. No, his little kitten would welcome him, and she'd be ready for him, and he ached, imagining how good it would feel to sink into her creamy satin heat.

But he wasn't going to just go to her every time he wanted release. She would assume his visits meant that he wanted her—not sex with her. She would imagine, as women did, that there was more to their relationship than a contractual marriage. She would then try to share things with him—thoughts and feelings—and expect him to reciprocate, and that wasn't going to happen. Ever. Better to disappoint her a little now than to risk greater drama later.

Kassiani had just finished dressing when a light knock sounded on the bedroom door. She opened it to discover one of the ship's stewards in the hall. "We have just anchored ⁓d Mr. Alexopoulos is waiting for you on the deck. He ⁓sts you bring a sweater." The steward glanced down at her feet. "He also suggested comfortable shoes but I think you'll be fine in those sandals. I'll wait for you here to show you the way."

"I'm ready now," she answered. "Let me just grab a sweater."

Kassiani was excited and also curious. She'd thought the yacht had slowed, and maybe stopped, but she hadn't realized they'd actually dropped anchor. "Where are we?" she asked as she followed the staff member down several flights of stairs to the level where they'd board a smaller boat.

"Paros," he answered simply.

"I've never heard of it," she answered truthfully.

As they stepped into the sunlight, Kassiani spotted her husband by the railing, and her stomach dropped amid a sudden flurry of nerves. He was tall and lean and quite devastatingly attractive this morning in a black knit shirt and khaki shorts that hit just above his knee. The shirt wasn't overly tight and yet even then it clung to his muscular shoulders and outlined the hard planes of his chest, while wrapping firm biceps, biceps that drew her attention.

He was far too handsome for her. She felt even dumpier as she joined him, only then noticing the sleek, white speedboat tethered to the side of the yacht. He extended a hand to her, to assist her into the boat. "We're having breakfast on shore."

"Good. I'm desperate for coffee," she answered, painfully self-conscious as she put her hand in his. In bed with him she'd felt confident, but yesterday had made her insecure again, and yet when his fingers closed around hers, she felt an electric shock and her shyness turned to heat, with disconcerting warmth flooding her limbs.

She wasn't sure if it was a good or bad thing that the racing boat made it virtually impossible to talk as they zipped across the water toward a whitewashed town flanking a gorgeous little bay. The shimmering buildings rose up on the hill and lined the small bay. "Tell me where we're going," she said as the boat slowed, approaching the wharf.

"We're going to spend the morning on Paros, one of my favorite Greek islands. Most tourists don't know about it, and yet it's only several hours by ferry from Athens. First we'll have breakfast in Naousa, the fishing village in front of us, and then we'll go explore for a bit before having a glass of ouzo and returning to the yacht."

She listened to this without comment, butterflies flitting madly in her middle as her gaze settled on his strong, muscular legs, his skin a warm burnished bronze. She'd thought he looked powerful and handsome in his wedding tuxedo, but this casual dress made her think wicked, carnal thoughts, thoughts where he had her naked on the bed, and he was doing the most wonderful things to her.

He took her hand again as they docked, his fingers interlacing with hers, and kept it as they entered town, traveling through narrow whitewashed alleyways with shutter-framed windows. Flowers spilled from huge glazed terra-cotta pots, and purple bougainvillea bloomed over doorways.

She didn't know where they were going, but he did, and they traveled through town, up a narrow cobblestone road to a building partway up the hill. It was a café, she discovered as they crossed the threshold, and a waiter came forward to greet them, escorting them to a table on the terrace with a view of the port.

"That was a hike," she said with a small laugh as they were seated. "Now I know why I needed appropriate shoes."

"Are your feet sore?"

"No. I'm good."

"It's a bit of a climb, but the view, and the food, is worth it."

Coffee and slender glasses of bright orange juice arrived, and then the waiter rattled off the menu options to them in Greek. Kassiani understood most of what the waiter said, and so when Damen turned to her to translate, she said she'd have the option of omelets.

After ordering, she glanced around, soaking in the scenery. The terrace wall was stone, and more pots of flowers and small trees dotted the patio. A half-dozen small wooden tables and chairs were scattered across the terrace, the chairs a lovely blue, and a perfect reflection of the turquoise water below.

Inside the café she could hear voices, but for the most part, it seemed as if they were the only customers.

"Why is no one else here?"

"I called ahead and reserved the terrace."

She laughed. "Why?"

He shrugged. "The tables are too close. I didn't want to risk others listening to us."

"Are you afraid we're going to fight?"

He gave her a puzzled look. "Why would we fight?"

She took a sip of her juice. "I suspected from your distance yesterday that you were upset with me."

He looked at her a long moment, and then glanced away. "Not upset, but I'm accustomed to space. I thought we could both use some space."

She returned her glass to the table. "This is off topic, but this is some of the best orange juice I've ever had."

"It's probably from Laconia or Argos."

"Well, it's delicious." She dabbed her mouth with her linen napkin and set it back on the table beside her plate before rising. "And with regards to space and independence, I'm very independent, but to be honest, I was concerned yesterday that I'd done something wrong on our wedding night, and that my inexperience left you disappointed."

"It didn't. You didn't."

That wasn't a good enough answer in her book. He'd been rude yesterday. He'd hurt her. And she didn't expect him to slather over her, but this was their honeymoon and a chance for them to get to know each other. "Because when I didn't see you yesterday, or hear from you in any way, it was logical to assume that I'd failed in my wifely duties."

He shrugged carelessly. "I don't know how else to re-assure you that you did not disappoint me. I enjoyed our wedding night, and I hope you did, too."

Any pleasure she might have felt in his words was di-minished by his cold, measured delivery. There was no warmth in him, and none of the passion of their wedding night.

Damen lifted a finger, signaling the waiter, indicating she wanted more juice since her glass was now half-empty.

She found it interesting that he couldn't give her any emotional warmth, but he'd make sure she had plenty to eat and drink. Did he imagine this was how good hus-bands behaved?

Apparently he did, because as soon as the waiter re-treated, Damen said bluntly, "I've been a bachelor for thirty-six years. I'm accustomed to my routine and doing things my way."

"Of course."

"Which means, we're not always going to see each other every day, and we won't be sleeping with each other every night."

"When you say *sleeping*, is that your euphemism for sex?"

"Yes."

"Interesting."

"I warned you I wouldn't be a tender husband. I tried to protect you from who I am. You didn't listen. You insisted you wanted this marriage. This is who I am."

"And who are you?"

"Hard. Cold. Indifferent to the needs of others."

She swallowed with difficulty, refusing to let herself be intimidated. "You weren't indifferent in bed."

Silence followed, so thick and heavy that Kassiani could barely breathe, and then he leaned forward, leaning so close that she could see the silver flecks in his gray eyes. "Sex is the only time I feel anything, and I prefer sex rough. I like to dominate. I enjoy the power. It turns me on."

No wonder he didn't want anyone around them.

Kass swallowed again, her face flushing, her body tingling, wondering why she wasn't scared as much as… aroused. "Fascinating. This is a new world to me. Do you like toys? Whips? Nipple clamps? Handcuffs?"

Damen pushed his coffee cup back, incredulous.

Kassiani might gaze innocently at him, all big brown eyes and sweet smiling lips, but he was beginning to discover that her placid cheerfulness hid a very sharp mind and an extraordinarily steely spine.

"No nipple clamps or whips yet," he answered, checking his testy tone, not wanting her to know just how much she tried his temper. "But there's a place for handcuffs, and the right toy."

Her cheeks turned an even darker pink but she held his gaze. "So since we're on our honeymoon, why wouldn't you want to have sex every night, with or without toys? Unless, you don't really want…me."

"I do want you." In fact, he'd like to bend her over the breakfast table and lift her pretty navy sundress and show her how good it felt when he took her from behind. He was certain he'd get more than a few pants and hoarse cries of pleasure. "But I don't need to have sex every night," he added, grateful the table with its blue-and-white linen cloth hid his lap and his thick, heavy erection.

"But do you want it?" she asked. "Every night?"

His jaw nearly dropped. Her questions astounded him. "I don't find it necessary to impose on my wife every night."

"Even if your wife wants your company in her bed?"

She might have been a virgin when he married her, but she wasn't an innocent. The woman was provocative as hell. "I don't spend the night with anyone. After sex, I always leave."

"Why?"

"Because that is how I prefer it." He ground down, jaw tightening. "It's not necessary for me to explain myself to you, and I'm not sure why I'm even trying."

"Maybe because your wife wants to get to know you, and seeks to understand you."

"There is nothing to understand. Some weeks we might have sex nightly. Other weeks we might have sex a couple times a week. It depends on my work schedule and my mood."

"So I'm not to initiate?"

A picture of her taking him in her mouth flashed through his head and burned all over, so hot he felt as if he might pop out of his skin. "I didn't say that."

"So if I want to sleep with you each night, I can approach you?"

And just like that, he hardened all over again, his shaft throbbing, aching to be freed. "You can't want it every night. In fact, I'm sure you don't want it every night. You've only just lost your virginity."

"The point is, what if *I* want you to come to see me at night? What if *I* want your company in my bed?"

"This isn't a love marriage. I'm not going to romance you."

"I don't believe I asked for romance."

Damen wasn't accustomed to being questioned, or challenged. No one questioned him and he couldn't quite believe she was now. What did she hope to gain? Was this some kind of ill-conceived marital test? "Are you some kind of sex fiend?" he drawled, deliberately using words he was sure would offend her. It was best to check her now, let her know that he wasn't her father, he didn't invite arguments or challenges. He was a traditional male, and he was expecting a traditional wife. Those were the terms of their marriage and she had agreed just the other night, promising to put his comfort before all else.

If he'd thought his offensive words would check her, he was wrong. Her eyes didn't well with tears. There was no quiver of her lower lip. Instead she held her place, lips curved, chin tilted, expression cheerfully defiant. "Would you be unhappy if I *was* a sex fiend?"

"You're not," he answered shortly, impatiently. "You were a virgin just the other night. The sheets bore witness to your lack of experience."

"But maybe I have tapped into long-suppressed desires. Or—" she paused, head tilted, expression thoughtful "—or, I have discovered how much I enjoyed being with you." She paused again, a dark winged eyebrow arching. "Or is that not allowed? Am I not to have any desire of my own? Am I to only serve you but not feel pleasure in our coupling?"

Damen ground his teeth together, beyond exasperated. She was pushing him, and hard, and this was only day three of their marriage. "You're not playing by the rules," he gritted.

Her winged eyebrow rose higher. "I should have realized you had rules. Because, of course, a man like you has *dozens* of rules, rules that can't be challenged. So list them now and we can be on the same page."

"You are not the meek, compliant woman you pretended to be."

"I never pretended to be meek, or compliant. If you recall, I fought for you, and I fought for our marriage."

The fact that she was right didn't improve his mood. "Are you goading me?"

"I just think it's time I heard your expectations."

Damen was holding on to his temper by a thread. "I expect my wife not to harass me."

She laughed. Out loud. And then she reached up and covered her mouth, her lush, ripe mouth that made him think of all the sinful things he wanted to do to her mouth. "I'm sorry," she apologized, and yet her dark eyes glinted, glimmering with fresh amusement. "I'll try not to laugh—"

"Not try. Do it."

"Right. I'm not to laugh, and I'm not to talk, and I'm just supposed to listen."

"About time," he muttered.

She crossed one leg over the other and smoothed the navy fabric of her skirt. Her gaze met his and her expression was more sober but a hint of amusement still lurked in the warm brown depths. "I'm ready."

He would ignore the bright light in her eyes, just as he'd ignore the flecks of gold that made her eyes so warm and beautiful. Her dark brown hair had the same bits of copper here and there. She reminded him of fire and veins of copper amid granite rock, and her strength coupled with her lush shape made him question everything he knew about women.

"I am not looking for a best friend, or even a friend," he said tersely, sounding to his own ears like an unlikable ogre, but it was the truth and he wasn't ashamed of it. "I am not looking for a partner. I live for my work, and when I need something personally, I reach out to have that need met, but once I have what I need, I am again content being left alone."

And then he stopped talking and silence stretched. Kassiani finally gave a short nod, her expression perfectly neutral. How she didn't look offended by his brusque delivery, he didn't know.

Their hot breakfast arrived, eggs with cheese and tomatoes and olives, along with some pan-fried potatoes. They ate in silence and drank their coffee in silence and only when they were finished and Damen was paying the bill did Kassiani speak again.

"How will I know when you want me?" she asked quietly, her smile tight. "I want to be sure I understand the signal. I would hate to impose when I'm supposed to be hidden, and out of your way."

He slipped the folded bills beneath the small plate, and then rose. "That's not what I said."

She rose, too. "No? Because from what I heard, my job description reads obedient, self-sufficient and, above all, convenient."

CHAPTER FIVE

SHE WAS SO glad to be out of the restaurant and moving, even if she didn't know where they were going. She let Damen walk in front of her, and she followed, not wanting to talk to him, wishing she could escape him, but that was unlikely since she didn't know where they were and hadn't brought any money with her, either.

A car was waiting at the foot of the cobblestone street, and it turned out the car was waiting for them. Damen opened the door for her and climbed in next to her.

As the car traveled away from town, she stared out the window, eyes prickling and burning. Despite the fact that it wasn't an overly warm day, she felt hot and flustered... *furious*, actually. She'd always thought her father was unkind and self-centered, but at the moment Damen made her father look like a jovial Santa Claus.

She was still seething when Damen pointed out a glimmering path in the distance. "The Byzantine Road," he said. "If we had more time, we could walk it. It's a marble path that connects the villages of Prodromos and Lefkes."

"What are we doing instead?" she asked.

"We're heading to Parikia, the island's capital. There are several really interesting places I thought you might enjoy, including a cathedral, a thirteenth-century Venetian castle, the Archaeological Museum Parou and an ancient cemetery, which has always drawn me. Not sure why."

It all sounded fascinating and Kassiani focused on the adventures ahead, and it was only later when they were end-ing their day with the glass of ouzo in a beachfront *taverna*, she realized that the way he'd described the attractions—a cathedral, a castle and cemetery—all sounded rather grand, but nothing in Parikia was grand at all. Even the museum was quite small. But the sites were interesting and she enjoyed visiting places that weren't teeming with tourists. The cemetery grounds were a bit overgrown, but the tombs and marble headstones were a testament to the antiquity of the cemetery.

As they sat with their glass of ouzo in the *taverna*, her gaze swept the little town with the cobblestone streets and gleaming white buildings with colorful blue painted doors and shutters. "It's a charming little town, but I think I'd go mad here," she said, turning back to Damen. "I'm afraid I've lived in a city too long. I wouldn't know what to do here."

"What did you do at home?"

"Visit museums. Go to the library. Walk along the waterfront. Read in Golden Gate Park."

"Who did you do those things with?"

"Myself."

"I'm sure you had friends."

"Not really."

"Why not?"

"Like you, I enjoy my own company. I don't need constant attention."

"But you were upset that I gave you space yesterday."

"A little reassurance after our wedding night would have been nice, but there's no point in rehashing that, is there?"

"I didn't mean to hurt you," he said tersely. "But I do think—" He broke off, shook his head. "I don't want to argue."

She didn't want to argue, either, and yet she did wish

to understand him. "Is it arguing if we are trying to clarify things?"

He reached out and captured her chin, turning her face to his. "Arguing is conflict. I don't do conflict."

She could feel the heat of each of his fingers against her jaw, and his voice had dropped, and his deep, husky tone sent a strangely delicious shiver up and down her back. "Because you're a traditional Greek man, or you just have an overwhelming need to dominate?"

"Just an FYI, kitten, you are neither obedient nor convenient."

His voice had grown even huskier, which sent a frisson of pleasure through her. "I'm sorry I can't please you."

His silver gaze warmed. "Perhaps you need to try a little harder."

"Perhaps you need to work with me a little more," she flashed. "Perhaps training a new wife takes more time than you anticipated."

"Is that where this has gone all wrong? I've failed to train you?"

There was a smoky promise in his words that made her heart thump and her insides melt. She pressed her knees together, excited. "You have deck crew, and a captain and an engineer. You have a chief officer, and a second officer and a third officer. A chase boat captain. An officer on watch. Bosun, security officers, purser, chief steward, a second steward, housekeeper, chefs, cooks, laundry and spa therapists—"

"I'm fully aware of all the staff I employ," he interrupted drily.

"But you haven't hired anyone to train me," she concluded. "Which means you either need to bring someone on board to teach me how to be a proper wife, or you'll have to do it yourself—"

He dropped his head, his mouth covering hers, silencing the stream of words, and when he lifted his head again, his gray eyes glittered and dark color stained his cheekbones. "It seems it's time to continue your training. We'll return to the ship now."

The speedboat was there in pretty Parikia Harbor as was the yacht, as they'd both traveled around the island to pick them up.

Kassiani tried to ignore her rapidly thudding pulse as they approached the yacht but Damen's words echoed in her head.

Time to continue your training.

"Am I in trouble?" she asked breathlessly as they boarded the yacht and Damen took her hand and led her up the flights of stairs to the master bedroom.

"Do you want to be in trouble?"

"I am a little nervous," she confessed.

He pinned her against the bedroom door. "Good." And then he kissed her again, a hot, demanding kiss that made her legs tremble and her heart race. He was, without a doubt, the most exciting thing that had ever happened in her life. By the time he lifted his head, hers was spinning and her heart was racing and it felt like she had honey wine in her veins.

"When we go inside, you're going to listen to me," he said. "You're not going to argue. You're going to do exactly what I tell you."

"Because it turns you on?"

"Yes." His lips brushed her cheekbone, and then near her ear. "And I think it turns you on, too." And then he reached down and twisted the doorknob, the bedroom door opening so abruptly she nearly fell into the room. He caught her by the elbow, righting her and steering her into the bedroom before closing the door hard behind them, and then locking it.

Her pulse hammered as he locked the door, and then the air left her lungs when he quietly commanded, "Take off your dress. I want to look at you."

Heat flooded her, and she could feel herself turning pink, the blood rushing from her chest, up her neck to burn her cheeks, but she headed to the windows to draw the curtains.

"What are you doing?" he ground out.

"Closing the curtains."

"Why?"

"Because someone might see."

He barked a laugh, the sound low and so husky that it sent a thrilling ripple through her. "Like me?"

"Perhaps," she answered, her voice quavering. Her voice wasn't the only thing shaking. She was trembling, but she wasn't afraid. No, she was aroused and she felt hot and wet and completely needy, but this was all still new to her and she couldn't help feeling timid and uncertain.

"You weren't shy the other night. Why be shy now?"

"It was night. The room was dark."

"All the better to see you clearly now."

Some of the warmth inside her faded. Air bottled in her chest. She struggled to keep her emotions in check. "I'm not Elexis."

"No? What a surprise."

"I'm serious."

"So am I. Take your dress off, Petra Kassiani. Your husband grows impatient."

Her eyes burned. Her throat threatened to seal closed. He would see just how plump she was. He'd be impossibly turned off. But collapsing into tears wouldn't help, nor would they protect her from his scorn. Maybe it was better to get this over with. Let him see just who and what he'd married. Summoning her courage, she reached down, gathered the skirt of her sundress in her hands and lifted it up, drawing the dress up over her head before dropping it on the floor next to her.

She stood in her navy lace bra and panties, the bra straps not dainty, because her breasts weren't dainty. At least the matching navy lace panties weren't large. They were cut low on the hip with high legs that tried to make the most of the figure she had.

She kept her head up as he studied her pale form in the sunlight. It was all she could do not to cover herself. Kassiani knew she had too many curves and not enough flat-toned places. Exercise did little to change her shape, too. But she wouldn't cower, and she wouldn't let him know how painful this was for her.

She needed their relationship to be successful. Yes, she'd come into an inheritance when she married Damen, her father's late sister having set up a trust fund for Kassiani when she was a young girl because Kassiani had reminded her aunt Calista so much of herself as a girl. And Aunt Calista had not had a happy life.

Aunt Calista had never married, and had lived trapped with her own family as a single woman, and she hadn't wanted that future for Kassiani, and so she'd created a trust for Kass, ensuring she'd inherit money at twenty-five, or when she married, so that she'd always have options and not be dependent on her family.

But her aunt Calista didn't understand that Kass wanted to be married, because she wanted children. She hadn't married Damen so that she could leave him and live off her trust fund. She'd married Damen to be a wife and mother, and maybe she didn't know how to be a traditional Greek wife, but she could be a good wife. She was determined to be what Damen needed. After twenty-three years of being shunned and invisible, she was ready to be seen.

"You are beautiful," Damen said abruptly, his deep, rough voice breaking the silence.

"I'm not—"

"You are. If you weren't, I wouldn't say it." He dropped onto the bed, and leaned back, watching her from beneath heavy lids. "Take off your bra."

Heat rushed through her, making her skin prickle, and her breasts tighten and peak. She reached behind her and unhooked the bra, peeling it off before discarding it on the floor on top of her dress.

"Now your panties," he directed.

"You're not making this very comfortable," she flashed.

"Good. That makes it even more stimulating."

"Why do you like dominating?" she asked, stepping out of her panties.

"Why do you like being dominated?"

"I don't."

"I think you do, and here is why. You're smart. You're smarter than anyone else in your family. They are all predictable. Your life has been predictable. It's unpredictable now, and you and your interesting brain like that."

She couldn't argue with that, and his insight astounded her. "Do you say this to all your women?"

"No. You're nothing like the women I've had in my life. You're like nothing I've ever known."

"Is that bad?"

"No. It's good. Now touch yourself," he interrupted. "Play with your nipples."

She stiffened, flushing. Her hands wrapped around her middle. "I can't do that."

"Why not?"

"That's just…weird. Awkward."

"But doesn't it feel good?"

"My breasts are awful. They are so big—"

"They're perfect. But as it makes you nervous being the only one naked, I'll disrobe, too, which should level the playing field slightly." He rose and removed his clothing.

Shirt, pants, snug briefs off, one after the other.

She gulped as his thick erection sprang free. He was big, and the head of his shaft was equally thick and round. He reached down and stroked the length of him, his palm giving extra attention to the smooth head.

She remembered him in her mouth, and remembered how he'd filled her, and how incredibly good it had felt when he'd thrust in and out, finding sensitive spots within her that she hadn't even known about.

"Now touch yourself," he said, sitting back down on the bed, his powerful thighs parted, his hand still on his erection.

He was bronze all over. He had no tan lines. Her mouth dried and she felt a wobble in her legs.

"Surely you, brilliant young thing, can follow a few basic instructions," he said, and yet his tone wasn't harsh, more amused than anything.

Her cheeks heated. She exhaled hard, her nipples tightening into aching points even as she began to throb between her thighs. "I have. I'm here, and naked."

"But you're not touching yourself."

"I can't."

"You could if you knew there were consequences for disobeying me."

"Like?"

"Tie you up, and leave you there all day, naked—"

"You wouldn't."

"Or tie you up and lick you but not let you come." He paused considering other punishments. "Would you prefer me to spank you? A sharp slap on your pretty ass and then a lovely warm rub?"

She pressed her knees together, growing wetter, feeling positively drenched. "If I touch myself now, will you do what we did the other night? I loved that. I loved being close to you. I'm too far away right now."

"You should be proud of your body. It's beautiful."

"It's thick—"

"Why do women assume men want to take scrawny bony sticks to bed? I think you have an astonishing figure."

"You really do?"

"I've been hard all day. I find everything about you incredibly appealing. Maybe too appealing."

"Is that possible?"

"Yes. I can't get work done if I'm thinking about you and being in you and making you come."

She dropped her head, shy, and yet also rather victorious. He'd been thinking about her? It was heady and empowering. "It's all I thought about yesterday."

"So my little kitten is a sex fiend."

Her head shot up and she looked at him, but he was smiling and his expression was warm. Far warmer than she'd ever seen from him.

"Maybe," she murmured, voice husky. "Because I do want you."

"Enough talking, then." He rose and crossed to where she stood, and carried her to the bed, where he half dropped her into the middle of the mattress. He moved over her, his knees parting her thighs, and then spreading them wider so that he could look down at her, and see all of her. "I do like you bare," he growled.

Her thighs trembled as his fingertip traced her cleft and then between her soft swollen folds.

"So wet," he said, voice dropping lower.

She closed her eyes as he dipped a finger into her and spread the moisture up over her, teasing the hooded nub. She felt her hips lift, and arch as he did it again. And then he was there at her entrance, and pushing into her, his shaft so warm, instantly making her feel hot, and impossibly connected to him.

Something happened when he was buried in her that made her want to hold on to him, and keep holding on, keeping him with her.

She wrapped her arms around his neck and drew him down, wanting to feel him against her breasts, wanting to inhale his scent, wanting his warmth all around her.

He said he was awful and didn't feel, but that wasn't true. He wasn't as hard as he said he was, and clearly, he did have feelings. Damen might say he didn't care, but actions spoke louder than words, and when he kissed her, a deep scorching kiss where his tongue took her mouth just as he took her body, he was warm and protective. All day he'd been attentive and protective, making her feel as if she truly was his.

In a strange way, she felt as if she was the one who was supposed to be here, not Elexis. Elexis would never understand him, but she could. She would. She liked puzzles and challenges, and she was good at reading not just text, but subtext. And when she and Damen were together like this, it felt rather like perfection in an imperfect world.

Together like this, she felt as if she belonged. She belonged with him. She belonged to him. For the first time in her life, she belonged somewhere.

Kassiani shattered just as Damen began to come, their bodies climaxing together, and she welcomed his last hard, driving thrust, accepting everything he had, and everything he could give her. He was home.

Moments passed, and Kassiani struggled to catch her breath, her thoughts cloudy, her body still floating.

Their wedding night had been incredibly satisfying, but the lovemaking just now, and the orgasm she'd had, was, well, life changing. She liked being with him, even when he was edgy and dangerous. No one had ever challenged her in her life. Until now.

She felt Damen shift, rolling onto his back, and he drew her against his chest. His skin was warm and slightly damp, and as she rested her cheek on his chest, she breathed him in. He smelled delicious. She inhaled the scent—man, sex and a spicy fragrance—and it crossed her mind that she needed to be careful. He was potent. She would need to guard her heart.

"How do you feel?" he asked, lightly stroking her back.

How did she feel? Amazing. Surely he knew that. She glanced up into his face, feeling rather lucky in that moment to have a husband who was famous for his shrewd business acumen and a threat in the boardroom, as well as gifted in the bedroom. "Good."

His hand continued the slow caressing of her back. His touch made her want to purr. "I hate that your family has treated you so shabbily. It makes me want to take your father apart, limb by limb."

She smiled crookedly, and stretched up to kiss him. "Please don't do that, but thank you for being my protector. I've never had one before."

"I'm not a hero."

"No, you're definitely more of a thug, but you're handsome as heck, so it works for you."

He laughed, softly. "You're one surprise after another."

"I hope that's a good thing."

"It is." He kissed her back, a hand threading into her

hair, and the kiss flared into something hot and bright. "I hate to go, but I need to."

"Why do you need to go?"

"I've been out of touch with the office all day. I'm sure there are dozens of emails and phone calls and matters awaiting my attention."

"Just stay a little longer. Stay and talk to me. Please?"

She could feel him tense and she stroked his chest. "There is so much I want to know about you. Tell me about your work and family, tell me about your first girlfriend, tell me—"

"That's an awful lot to cover in five minutes."

"Okay, then forget all that. Just answer this. Have you ever been in love?"

He hesitated. "No."

"That wasn't very convincing."

He didn't reply.

"So you have been in love," she persisted.

Damen sat up and rolled to the side of the bed. "The less you know about me, the better. Knowing more about me would just lead to disappointment. I'm good at what I do because I'm focused and ruthless. I've perfected the art of not caring about others, or what they think."

"That can be a good thing in business."

"It's who I am all the time. I don't have different sides. Whether at work, or home, I'm the same. Unfeeling. Driven. Relentless."

She considered this a moment. "I don't think you are all that. If you were, you wouldn't care about what I want or need, and you wouldn't take such good care of me in bed."

"That's bed."

"Or on the island today."

"Don't make too much of it."

"It's more kindness and attention than I've had from anyone, ever."

Damen reached for her and rolled her onto her back, his big body angling over hers. "Don't say such things. It makes me hate your family even more."

She reached up to brush his thick black hair back from his brow. "Don't hate them. Hate is such a useless emotion."

"Hate can be powerful."

"You don't need hate, and you don't need more power."

His light gaze locked with hers and he stared intently into her eyes. "So what do I need, then, Little Miss Know-It-All?"

"Maybe just how to be happy?"

"Because you're so happy?"

"I'm happier than I have been in a very long time."

"Because you're away from your family."

"Because I'm with you."

He made an incredulous sound and climbed off the bed. "Now you're playing me for a fool."

She sat up, drawing the light crisp sheet with her to cover herself. "Why can't I like you?"

"Because we don't have that kind of marriage. This is not a love marriage—"

"I know. And I said like, not love," she flashed irritably as he yanked on his clothes, first his shorts and then his shirt. "And right now, you're being ridiculous but that doesn't mean I don't still find you likable."

"That is not part of our agreement."

"I'm sorry."

"If you're sorry, why are you smiling?"

"Maybe because you look really handsome right now."

He growled his frustration. "I'm not handsome right now, and I'm not likable, and we don't have that kind of marriage, either."

"What kind is that?"

"The kind where everybody is happy and dreams come true." He turned and gave her a dark, tortured look. "You're a smart woman. You of all people should know that happiness is a myth and dreams are just that. Dreams."

CHAPTER SIX

HE'D SPENT ALL day with Kassiani today. Damen couldn't remember when he'd last spent four hours with anyone, never mind a woman.

And he'd enjoyed almost every minute. The only minutes he hadn't enjoyed were the minutes where she'd tried to convince him he was a good person, when he knew the truth about himself.

Kassiani. She was something of a revelation.

He'd known very little about her before their wedding, other than she was the youngest daughter, and a rather mysterious figure in her family, one her father had portrayed as eccentric, which was apparently why she didn't travel with them, and wasn't paraded about like Barnabas and Elexis. But now Damen could see that Kassiani had been forgotten and ignored by her family because she wasn't like them—she wasn't shallow and superficial. She didn't take advantage of people. She didn't use others. She actually thought of others.

Thank God her family hadn't corrupted her, but at the same time, she'd deserved so much better from her family. A great disservice had been done to Kassiani all these years. She actually believed she was fat and unattractive. Unworthy.

It was wrong.

And now he was handling her wrong, too, but Damen didn't know how to be a better husband. He wasn't accustomed to being patient or kind. So maybe that was the first step. Practicing patience. And maybe a little bit of kindness.

If Kass was surprised to see him on deck before dinner, she gave no indication. She was standing at one of the railings on the upper deck, and she turned her head to smile at him. "Good evening."

"Good evening to you. Have you been up here long?"

"Fifteen or twenty minutes. It's such a gorgeous night. The view is spectacular. The island ahead of us sparkles with light."

"That's Mykonos."

Her brow creased. "Weren't you and Elexis supposed to visit Mykonos?"

"We were, yes."

"Are we?"

"No." He saw the searching look she gave him. He shrugged. "I don't want to take you where I was going to take Elexis. It seems wrong somehow."

"It's okay. I've been there. It's fine, but it's not my favorite island."

"Which is your favorite island? Wait, let me guess. Santorini."

She grinned. "It's everyone's favorite, isn't it?"

"It's certainly picturesque." He turned from the view of Mykonos to face her. "How did you know about the honeymoon plans?"

"Elexis asked me to read through the itinerary and make sure she would like it."

His jaw dropped slightly. "And did you?"

Her shoulders twisted. "It gave me something to do."

"And you like to be helpful."

"I like having a sense of purpose, yes. It's frustrating to me that I've gone to school and have a degree and yet my father refuses to allow me to work outside the home."

"So you've never held a job?"

"Charity work. That's about it."

"And your brother and sister?"

"The same. Although Barnabas was supposed to work with Dad once he finished university, only he never finished university because his grades were so bad."

"How does he get his money?"

"Dad transfers money each month into Barnabas's bank account."

"Why?"

"I guess it's like an allowance."

"Your brother is twenty-eight years old. Isn't that a little old to be getting an allowance?"

"Dad is afraid that if he cuts Barnabas and Elexis off financially, they'll cut him out of their lives. And he couldn't bear that, so he gives them whatever they want."

"So you get an allowance, too?"

"No." Her voice was sharp and her smile brief. "I get nothing other than a roof over my head and the food I eat."

"Why the double standard?"

"Barnabas and Elexis tell Dad what he wants to hear. I don't."

"What do you tell him instead?"

"That the company needs more leadership, and the family shouldn't be sponging off the company. Dukas Shipping isn't there to be the personal bank account for lazy family members that don't want to work."

Damen's eyebrows shot up. "You've said all this?"

"And more."

His lips twitched. "I can't imagine he valued the input."

"Not at all, but he values his business, and I'd be wrong to remain silent when so much is at stake. It could be such an incredible company—"

"It will be, once I'm completely in charge."

"Are you removing my father as president and CEO?"

"He hasn't actively managed the company in years. He knows I'll be taking over after the honeymoon." He shot her a swift side-glance. "Does that upset you?"

"I'm relieved, actually. Something has to be done. I just…" She sighed, shrugged. "Never mind."

She turned away from him to stare out over the water and he used the moment to study her elegant profile. She truly was beautiful, with the regal features of a Greek goddess. "Tell me," he said quietly. "Finish the thought. I want to hear it."

She glanced at him, eyes bright, lips compressed. "If I was a son, he would have made room for me. I would have been an asset. Instead I was a daughter and nothing but a disappointment."

Before he could reply, one of his stewards appeared with the champagne he'd requested twenty minutes ago and made a big production about opening the bottle and filling their flutes.

Damen checked his temper as the steward settled the champagne bottle into the ice bucket, rattling the ice as if he was doing the most important job in the world. Finally the steward was gone and Damen handed Kassiani a flute.

"We didn't have a toast on our wedding night. So, *stin yeia sou*," he said, lifting his glass. *To your health.*

"Yamas," she answered, to *our* health, before clinking the rim of her goblet to his and lifting her flute to her lips.

Just watching her bring her glass to her full lips made him hard. He didn't understand this fascination with her, or why he found it so hard to stay away from her. She was so naturally sensual that she had him in a constant state of arousal.

"What else have you told your father that he doesn't want to hear?" Damen asked, determined to shift his attention from her luscious mouth to the topic they'd been discussing before the champagne had arrived.

"Dukas Shipping was worth so much more five years ago, when my father first approached you. He's been cutting away into the principal. You've gotten a rotten deal. Instead of the Dukas beauty, you got the Ugly Duckling *and* a company teetering on bankruptcy."

"You wanted to work for him."

"Desperately." She swallowed hard. "I have tried for years to get him to bring me on board. I even told him he didn't have to pay me. I'd be an intern. Just let me go to the office and give me a chance to learn the ropes."

"Is it true you studied business and international relations at Stanford?"

"It is true."

"That couldn't have been an easy course of study."

"It was actually not that difficult. I read quickly, and have one of those memories that forget nothing." Her lips quirked. "It's a blessing and a curse."

"So you've been out of school a couple years."

"Four years end of this month. I started Stanford at sixteen and finished the dual major in three years."

Very little surprised Damen, but she'd just caught him completely off guard. "Most Americans don't start university until they're what…eighteen?"

"I tend to do accelerated studies. I can take more classes than most students. The workload isn't a problem for me." She grimaced. "More of that blessing and a curse."

"Have you ever been tested? Are you considered gifted?"

"I have, and I am. But I wish I wasn't. My mother wasn't particularly intellectual and she used to say that brainy women were objectionable as they tended to challenge the status quo, competing with men rather than allowing the man to feel like the man."

"She wasn't a feminist."

"No."

"Little wonder your father adored her. Greek men expect to be the center of the world."

"Yes, I know." She hesitated. "It's why my aunt never married. She was brilliant, and smart, and strong, and her parents were traditional Greeks, and they didn't know what to do with her." She tapped the rim of her flute. "I think it's why she created the trust for me. She recognized a kindred spirit and wanted to be sure I had...options."

Her tone, and the bittersweet twist of her lips, made his chest tighten. Kassiani was a constant source of surprise. "What else did your mother teach you?"

"That beauty is a woman's greatest strength and virtue, and a socially inept woman was nothing short of a failure."

"Oh, dear."

"Mmm. In my parents' eyes, I've been a failure my entire life. Not attractive, and a social misfit. How could I be such a blight on the Dukas name?"

"Did you feel awkward at Stanford?"

"No. I loved being in school. I enjoy academia. I'm comfortable in certain environments, but hopeless in others. Like parties. I'm not comfortable at parties. I'm not good with chitchat. I'm the least fashionable woman you'll ever meet—"

"Oh, now, I'm not sure you can claim that honor. My mother only wears smocks, and these slipper-like shoes, with socks. It's terrible. Really. So, I think she has you beat."

Kassiani gurgled with laughter and Damen was pleased. He'd meant to make her laugh, and was glad he'd succeeded. He'd hated the pain in her voice, her pain making his chest tighten, and his temper stir. How dare her father treat her so shabbily all these years? How dare her parents make her feel less than something when she was the greatest Dukas of them all?

"Besides," he added after a moment, "fashion and parties are overrated. I would much rather have a brilliant wife than one who merely looked good in clothes."

For a moment there was just silence and Kassiani stared out over the water, toward the island glittering with light. Damen congratulated himself for soothing Kassiani's fears, and then she turned her head and looked him square in the eye. "Then why did you want Elexis in the first place? Why didn't you want...*me*?"

Her voice was calm, her tone thoughtful. It took him a second to realize she wasn't accusing him of anything, or trying to guilt him. She genuinely wanted to know.

Again his chest tightened and he felt a wave of remorse, and pain. She deserved so much better from all of them.

"You were never presented as an option," he said at length. "I didn't know enough about you to think to ask for you."

"You didn't realize there were two Dukas daughters?"

"Vaguely. You were, how shall I say? Mysterious."

"Kassiani, overly fond of math, burdened by a photographic memory." Her lips lifted in a wide, self-mocking smile. "Most mysterious indeed."

The moonlight bathed her in a lovely glow, illuminating her profile with her strong, elegant features. She was wearing a white dress with ruffles and flounces and it crossed his mind that while the white paired well with her dark hair and complexion, the flounces and frills were too much for her petite build, overwhelming her curves, adding to them, making her look bigger than she was. Kassiani was actually quite small physically. She just had exceptional curves, amazing curves, like Hollywood stars of old.

"You should be proud of your exceptional abilities and talent, not ashamed," he said.

"Do you think my father should have hired me?"

"I do."

Her gaze found his again, her expression somber. "Would you hire me?"

Damen straightened, feeling sucker punched. What a question. How could he answer that without becoming a villain, like her father? "I've hired a number of women for management positions. There is also a woman on my board."

"Out of what? Twelve?"

He didn't answer since they both knew the answer. Kassiani didn't pull punches, did she? Damen was beginning to understand why Kristopher preferred not to deal with his youngest. "The Greek shipping business is dominated by men, and in general, it isn't very receptive to women in key positions."

Kassiani sipped her champagne thoughtfully. Her silence felt like a condemnation and Damen didn't enjoy feeling judged.

"I didn't say I agreed with the attitude," he added somewhat defensively, and then felt angry about being made to feel defensive. "Men just want to get things done without all the emotional baggage women bring to the table."

She shot him a look of surprise that quickly morphed into one of disappointment and Damen gripped his flute so hard he was certain it would shatter.

"I had no idea you were one of those," she said calmly with just a hint of censure. "For some reason I thought you were more…progressive."

"Business is business," he said curtly. "I don't spend long hours at the office because I enjoy sitting at my desk. I'm there to get things done."

"And women don't get things done at the office?"

"You're twisting this, you know. You are deliberately twisting my words. But to answer your last question, this is exactly what I don't want in my office. I don't want to spar with a woman over real or perceived slights. I want to execute contracts. I want financial growth. I want to develop markets. What I don't want is to be challenged on my domain. It's not conducive to company morale—"

"Or yours," she interjected softly.

He broke off, frustrated, and rather furious, because this entire conversation had flipped. A couple of minutes ago they were having a really good and open conversation and now it was antagonistic. Why? What had happened?

And before he could answer that question, he had a sudden insight into why Kristopher had chosen to leave Kassiani at home, behind.

It wasn't because she was dumpy and dull. It wasn't because she was the proverbial Ugly Duckling. It was because Kristopher didn't know how to manage his youngest daughter. Kassiani was too smart for him, and probably talked circles around him, and Kristopher—not the brightest of men—couldn't cope. The only way he knew how to handle her was by shaming her.

Marginalizing her.

Making her feel small and less than.

Damen didn't agree with Kristopher's behavior, but he felt an unexpected surge of sympathy for the older man. Kristopher knew exactly what to do with Elexis and Barnabas—indulge them, give them money and toys. But Kassiani couldn't be bought off so easily. She was young, smart and fierce, honest and real.

"You know, kitten," he said quietly, "if you want to be part of the game, you have to play the game."

"Is there a game, then?"

Damen flashed back to Adras, and the horrors of being a young male trapped in a situation beyond his control, forced to do and say things that still made him physically ill. He knew then, at fourteen and fifteen, he'd never forgive himself, and he hadn't, even though twenty-two years had passed. "If you feel like you're always on the losing side, I'd say there is a game in play."

"And if I'm tired of losing?"

"Then figure out the game."

Dinner was strained that evening and Kassiani knew she was to blame—not because she was wrong, but because she couldn't remain silent on issues. Growing up, she'd never been able to accept the status quo, and she realized early on that what was acceptable in one family wasn't going to be acceptable in hers. Her family was old-world. Traditional. And if her feminist opinions weren't welcome at home in San Francisco, she should know they'd be a problem here in Greece.

Back in her bedroom, she kicked herself for not being able to hold her tongue. It had changed their evening. Damen had been in a good mood when he had joined her on the deck and had champagne delivered, and then she had to ruin the lovely champagne toast by being too pointed, and too direct, creating conflict, which was so typical of her.

Kass didn't know why she couldn't stop when she was ahead. If only she could harness the frustration she felt at not being given more opportunity.

The narrowness of her life wore on her.

The lack of challenges made her feel somewhat desperate and crazy.

She read half a dozen international newspapers a day, and tried to stay busy by digging in deeper into current events, researching current topics in world economics, international politics and international law. She subscribed to various university magazines, wanting to know what was happening in the academic world, as well as the corporate world. But all the research in the world did little to alleviate her sense of isolation.

But Kass didn't feel isolated when Damen claimed her, and made love to her. Kass didn't feel like a failure when he responded to her in bed. She wasn't a radical feminist. She didn't think of herself as a rabble-rouser. But Kass had always struggled with remaining silent when confronted by injustices. Women really were capable of so much.

And she, personally, was capable of so much more.

Maybe her need to be heard and seen…to contribute… was based on the fact that she didn't feel valuable as a decorative object. How could she? She wasn't very decorative. She added little value in terms of physical beauty. The only time she truly felt attractive was when she was using her brain.

Or using her body to seduce Damen.

She smiled weakly, ruefully. At least she still had her sense of humor. It wasn't appreciated in her family but Kassiani had always been grateful she could laugh at herself. Far better than always crying over one's faults and failings.

The door to the master bedroom opened. Kass jerked her head up, and her heart fluttered as Damen stepped into the room and closed the door behind him.

Suddenly the tears she'd been holding back fell and she reached up to swipe them away, one after the other before he could see.

"Why the tears?" he asked, standing at the foot of the bed.

So she hadn't successfully hid them. She sat taller and swiftly swiped away another, scrubbing at her cheeks to make sure they were now dry. "I didn't think you were going to come tonight. I thought I'd chased you away."

"So you don't believe what you were saying?"

"No, I do."

"Then don't apologize. Your problem is that you're smarter than everyone else."

She sniffed and swiped away a last tear. "Not smarter than you."

"I wouldn't say that. You are certainly book smarter. To be fair, I probably have you beat when it comes to street smarts."

She settled her nightgown over her knees, and exhaled slowly, trying very hard to bridge whom she was with what a wife was supposed to be. It was a tricky balancing act. "All right, so I don't apologize for having opinions, but I am sorry if I upset you at dinner. Trying to be a good wife is more complicated than I imagined."

"Why shouldn't you speak freely? I do."

She exhaled in a painful rush, her cheeks heating. "We both know the answer to that."

"Because men can, and women can't?"

"You've told me that my value lies in me being a supportive wife, not a critical, oppositional one."

"I actually don't think I ever told you that," he said mildly.

"A traditional Greek wife—"

"Isn't what I asked for. It's what you said I needed, because apparently I need a meek, submissive wife." He arched a black brow. "Now, there are things I would enjoy from a submissive wife, but it would probably not be what you're thinking."

Or would it? She silently countered, as unbidden images came to mind, images of her kneeling before him, worshipping his body, drawing his thick shaft into her mouth, sucking, licking, making him groan and slide a hand into her hair, his fingers wrapping around the strands, holding her head so that he could take his pleasure.

Kassiani exhaled again, her body hot, her senses stirred. Flustered, she pushed back a heavy wave of hair from her face, feeling overly warm, and more than a little claustrophobic, because suddenly the atmosphere felt charged, the air heavy, crackling with awareness, and desire.

She could tell that Damen felt the tension, too, as the look he gave her was blatantly sexual, as was his slow, possessive perusal, his gaze resting on the jut of her breasts and then lower to the swell of her hips and then finally to the hem of her nightgown where it clung to her thigh.

"Let me see you," he said slowly, arms folding over his chest.

"What do you want to see?"

"Everything."

"Then let me see you."

"What do you want to see?"

"Everything."

He laughed softly and gave his dark head a shake. "You are a fearless negotiator. I admire that." The corner of his mouth lifted. "Now let's see how good you are at asking for something. What do you want, Petra Kassiani? What would be your pleasure?"

She hesitated, thinking. "Something new. Something we haven't done. But something *I* would like," she added quickly, fighting her blush.

"Oh, that's easy, then. I haven't even taken you from behind yet. I think you'll like that position very much."

CHAPTER SEVEN

HE WAS RIGHT. She did like that position very, very much.

She was still trying to catch her breath after the most intense orgasm of her life, and Damen was stretched out next to her, his hand lightly running over her back, caressing from her back to her butt, and then up again.

Part of her was so relaxed but another part of her was already being stirred.

"Tell me something about your boyhood," she murmured, trying to distract herself. "Do you have brothers and sisters?"

"None. I was an only child."

"Why?"

"There were complications during my birth. My mother was lucky she and I both survived the pregnancy."

"That's scary."

"I am sure if we lived someplace else, and had easier access to doctors, it might have been less dangerous."

"You were poor."

"Very."

She curled closer to him, her arm wrapping around his waist. "And yet you have so much now."

"I made a vow when I was fifteen that I would never be poor again, and it's driven every decision I've made since then."

"What did your father do?"

"He worked in an olive orchard. My mother did, too. They earned so little that they couldn't afford child care for me, so from the very beginning I went to work with them, first strapped to my mother's back as an infant, and then later I ran about, trying to help. I didn't actually get paid until the year I turned ten. That was a big deal for me, and my family. It wasn't much compared to what my father earned, but it helped."

She pressed her hand to his chest, just above his heart. They'd had such different backgrounds, such different lives, and yet here they were together. "When did you find time to go to school?"

"I went seasonally. When I wasn't needed in the groves or the olive press."

"It doesn't sound like you had a lot of formal education, then."

"I attended off and on until I was fourteen—" He broke off, jaw hardening, brow darkening. "And that was the end of my boyhood. I never went back to school, and within eighteen months, I left our island, Adras, for good."

"Where did you go?"

"Athens. I got a job in the dockyards and worked hard, and here I am."

"How does a relatively uneducated boy become…you?"

"Relentless ambition." He smiled grimly. "And the desire for revenge."

She pushed up on her elbow to get a better look at his face. "Revenge? Why?"

"When you are poor, you are dependent on others." His jaw flexed. "There is a terrible imbalance of power."

She frowned. "What happened?"

"It's nothing I discuss. It's just…fuel. Anger and desperation are remarkable motivators."

"Why won't you tell me?"

"It doesn't matter anymore," he answered carelessly, his voice hardening. He sat up and kissed her forehead. "And now I just like working hard. Work gives me a reason to wake up every day. It gives satisfaction at the end of the day." He glanced at the bedside clock. "I'm actually hungry. Are you?"

"Hasn't your chef gone to bed?"

"No one sleeps if I want something," he said so matter-of-factly that she smiled.

And then he smiled, too, as if amused by his own arrogance. "All I want is a snack," he added, "and half the fun of a snack is going through the refrigerator and pantry to see what you can find."

The kitchen was surprisingly large with an enormous center island dominating the middle of the room. The backsplash, refrigerators, stove, ovens, even the four portholes above the prep area, all gleamed silver, while the cabinets were a rich espresso and the counters a creamy ivory marble shot with veins of pale caramel.

It was a beautiful space, and welcoming. Kassiani ran her hand over one of the lovely marble work surfaces. "This is a gorgeous kitchen. I wouldn't mind cooking in here. The kitchen on our family yacht isn't half as nice. For one, there are no windows or portholes, and for another, it's a rather hideous vanilla-and-stainless mix, and not pretty stainless like this, but restaurant grade and very commercial looking. This is like something you'd see in a stunning house."

"My chef is picky. He wouldn't come on board if he didn't have the right appliances and utensils and work space."

"You must like your chef quite a bit, then. My father fired staff right and left. He had no qualms replacing them."

"Most of my staff have been with me for a while now. There are a few new faces on this sailing, but the majority have been on my payroll for years. I'm happier surrounded by familiar staff, people I know I can count on."

Kassiani was surprised. She'd gotten the impression that

Damen wasn't attached to anyone, or anything. "Do you spend that much time on your yacht to keep everyone fully employed, then?"

"Half of the crew only work here on the yacht, while the other half work for me in another capacity. My chef here is also my chef in Athens. I just steal him from the house and bring him on board. Some of the housekeeping staff are also from Athens. Three of the hands work on my Adras estate, while others are from my Sounio villa."

"So are those your main homes?" she asked as he opened the refrigerator and began pulling out cheese after cheese, as well as a plastic container filled with washed fruit. "Athens, Sounio and Adras?"

He moved to a cabinet and found plates and silverware. "I have an apartment in London, but I haven't been in years. Too busy working to travel." Damen deftly arranged place settings in front of them before going to the tall narrow pantry and retrieving a set of pottery jars she suspected were filled with olives.

The jars of olives joined the cheese and fruit. Damen lifted the lid on one jar and, using a tiny wooden fork, reached in to pluck out a tiny, dark green olive. He held the olive to her mouth in an offering, and she took it, licking her lower lip to capture the droplet of olive oil. "Delicious," she said.

"Some people call these Cretan olives, but we also grow them on Adras."

He reached into another jar, and stabbed a small light green olive. "These are *nafplion*. One of my favorites. The texture is firm and a little crunchy, and the flavor is even better. Slightly nutty, slightly smoky. These are a true table olive and perfect with a sprinkle of lemon juice and bit of dill."

She plucked the offered olive from the wooden fork and

popped it into her mouth. He was right. It was a little bit crunchy and deliciously salty and somewhat nutty. "That is amazing," she said.

"There is nothing better than olives and bread. Now we just need bread." He turned around, his gaze narrowing as it swept the kitchen. Everything was so tidy. There was no food out anywhere on the counters. "Chef used to have a bread box where he kept the loaves, and the leftovers, but I don't see it."

"I'll have a look," she offered.

And as she moved past him to search the pantry, he caught her by the neck, his hand wrapping around her nape, and drew her to him.

Kassiani felt a jolt of electricity as his head dropped and his lips covered hers. She felt another sharp surge of sensation as his mouth moved across hers. He was hungry and he parted her lips, claiming her mouth, making her weak in the knees.

She always responded to him, and desire washed through her, hot and needy, her body softening against him, her arms reaching up to wrap his neck and bring him even closer. Damen held her firmly and she relished the feel of his hard, warm, muscular body pressed to hers as well as the seductive promise of his shaft urgent against her belly.

Nothing in her life had prepared her for this heat and desire. This physical need matched her emotional need, creating a vast yearning for more. Being in Damen's arms made her feel powerful and vulnerable at the same time, and she wanted to be completely herself, and completely real. Was this love? Or was this lust? She didn't know. She wished she knew. She wished she'd had more experience because what she felt with Damen was incredible and consuming and she couldn't imagine ever feeling this way with anyone else. It was as if he had been made for her. His body was extraordinary, and the way he used his body was extraordinary. She loved his scent, his skin and the very shape of him.

Kassiani hated it when she disappointed him. She hated it even more when he hurt her, but she'd come to crave time with him. Truthfully, her day only really began once she saw him. The only hours that were important were the hours with him, and the only hours she felt truly alive were the hours in his company. Was that normal?

What was this terrible need she felt for him?

Kassiani slid her hands under his shirt, relishing the texture of his hot skin. She wanted her mouth on him. All of him. She wanted to wrap herself around him and never let go. Damen leaned her back against the marble counter, exposing her neck and throat. His lips traveled the length of her jaw, lighting fire beneath her skin. She whimpered, and whimpered again as his teeth scraped a sensitive place on her neck that made her desperate for more. Her whimpers always stirred him, and he growled against her throat, his hips pressing against hers, and then his knee was between her thighs, his knee grinding against her, driving her wild.

She felt wild now.

"Security cameras," he panted, peeling away from her to go punch buttons into a box on the wall. "Don't need to give everyone a show."

She smiled, answering breathlessly, "It would be a good show."

"You are shocking."

"But you like it," she flashed, as he closed the kitchen door, locking it before returning to her side. "You like that I can't get enough of you."

They made love on the marble island counter. Damen

took her in so many different ways. Kass prayed the kitchen was soundproof because tonight he took advantage of those jars of olives and the accompanying olive oil to feast off her, dribbling the oil across her breasts and down her tummy to her thighs. After he made her come with his mouth, the oil became a massage, and then a lubricant and used for an exploration of her most sensitive, private places. Each orgasm was more intense than the last, and the pleasure so overwhelming that there were moments where she thought she would break down and cry, and she did end up crying after the last orgasm, the intensity of the intimacy making tears fall. She didn't even know why she was crying, only that she felt spent, and turned inside out. Her body didn't hurt, but she felt him everywhere even now when he wasn't in her. She felt his imprint and felt his possession and so the tears came and she tried to hide them from him, but he gathered her to him and held her, her body slippery and shuddering against his.

"I'll get oil all over you," she choked.

"I already have oil all over me."

"We're a mess."

"Chef is going to have to sanitize this center island tomorrow."

She laughed unsteadily and Damen used the pads of his thumbs to wipe beneath her eyes.

"I think I push you too far," he said, drawing her back against him so that her head rested against his chest. "I fear I am too much for you sometimes."

"You haven't broken me."

"I'm not trying to hurt you," he said hoarsely. "That's the last thing I would ever want to do to you."

She lifted her head to look up at him. "But you like the forbidden."

"This is true."

"So how far is too far?"

"That is up to you. I suppose I push you to see where you will draw the line."

"I don't want to draw lines between us. I don't want walls and boundaries. I want to trust you," she said softly, breathing in the scent of his skin, nearly always comforted by his nearness and the warmth of his skin. It was in these moments where she could hear his heart, and feel him relax, that she felt most comfortable, and safe.

Despite the unpredictable quality of the lovemaking, Damen felt like hers, and he still felt like home, and she couldn't remember a time, or place, or person who had felt like home...until now.

She kissed the side of his neck, and then the upper plane of his chest. "My goal is to trust you," she whispered, "so *you* can also trust *me*."

She felt him stiffen and she loosened her arms, but didn't let him go.

His hands smoothed over her arms, a caress to her upper arm, before carefully, deliberately peeling her hands away from his shoulders. "Do not take this the wrong way, but it will be years before I trust you. I find trust a very difficult thing. It's why when I find the right staff, I keep them. I pay them well and reward their loyalty because it's vital I retain them. Turnover makes me uneasy. I like to know who is true."

"Then I hope you will discover that I can be trusted, and not because I am your wife but because I care about you."

He let her hands fall and he pulled away, taking several steps back, putting distance between them. His features hardened, his expression had shuttered. "I don't need those words. I don't respond to those words. I would prefer not to say things like that in the future. If you don't mind."

Kassiani blinked, confused. "I don't understand."

His broad shoulders twisted carelessly. "I don't trust strangers. I don't trust people in general. And I most of all do not trust words. Your actions will matter to me more than anything you can say. So please do not use words of affection here. Don't say I care for you. I don't believe it. I will never believe it. Just show me with your actions that you are a loyal wife, and with time your actions will reveal the truth."

A knot formed in her throat, matching the knot in her chest. His voice had become brittle and icy cold. His features looked as if they'd been carved from stone. This harsh, unfeeling man frightened her a hundred times more than their edgy sex games.

When he spoke so disparagingly about love and affection, it made the fine hair on her nape rise, and her stomach cramp, and her survival instinct scream at her to run. But run where? Go where? He wasn't a date. He wasn't a boyfriend. He was her husband. She had to make this work. She had to find a middle ground. "We have been spending a lot of time together," she said quietly, calmly, trying to keep her voice even and reasonable. "It's only natural that I will develop feelings—"

"No," he interrupted sharply. His jaw flexed, his body tensed. "No," he repeated more quietly. "Feelings are not natural to me. I find 'feelings' suspect, particularly any that you might have for me. Why would you have feelings for me? I don't give you affection. I am not tender in bed. I use you as I use my mistresses. I'm hard, and demanding, and when I take you I…"

She flinched at his words, but refused to look away.

"I warned you that first night. I said I was hard. I am hard. And it gives me pleasure to be ruthless. It turns me on—"

"Yes, I know. You've made that abundantly clear," she

said coolly, impatiently, masking her frustration and hurt. "But just because you like sex a certain way doesn't make you a bad person."

"But I am a bad person."

"I'm sorry, but I see no evidence of that, anywhere."

"Oh, no?" he retorted, in that deep, rough, unapologetic voice, before running his hand across the firm, carved plane of his chest, sweeping the sheen of oil lower, over his chiseled abdomen, and then down to his cock, which was thick and hard and fully erect. "Would a tender groom do this? Would he enjoy shocking his bride? Wouldn't a good man try to be a gentleman in front of his bride?"

She shrugged. "I don't know. I don't really care. What I care about is you, and me, and you don't intimidate me, and you don't threaten me. You're my husband."

"Then you're not as smart as I thought you were, because I'm dangerous, kitten, I am destructive. You should be careful around me. And you should be careful about what you feel, because if I were you, I wouldn't trust me. I know who I am, and I know what I am, and I'm not safe."

His words made her go hot, and then cold. She didn't understand how he could go from sensual and passionate to volatile and destructive, but she knew this—she wouldn't stand here and listen to this. For one, she didn't believe it, and she wasn't going to buy into the fact that he was some treacherous monster.

Kass turned, searching for her clothes, and then remembered she'd come to the kitchen with him just wearing her nightgown. She couldn't imagine putting the silk gown on now, not over the oil covering her body. It would ruin it, stain it. She liked this pretty nightgown too much to ruin it. She wasn't the type to be careless with her things.

Or her people.

She clamped her jaw tight, grinding her teeth together

to keep her emotion in check, as she grabbed his shirt from the ground, and stuffed her arms into the long sleeves. He was tall and his shirt had plenty of fabric and it covered her better than most of her sundresses. Once dressed, she scooped up her nightgown, pushed her hair back from her face and faced him, her expression smiling but fierce.

"Thank you for your attention, and your helpful advice," she said. "I've made a mental note of your wishes, but just as I can't control you, you can't control me, and I shall care for whomever I want—"

"I don't want feelings in our relationship."

"Desire noted. I shall do my best to refrain from expressing emotion so that our sexual encounters be more like the ones you enjoyed with your mistresses. Now please unlock the door and let me return to my room."

Kass tossed and turned all night, too upset to sleep well. She was so angry with Damen. And if he thought he could bully her into submission, he was wrong.

He had no idea who she really was, or what she was made of, and she hadn't survived life in the Dukas household to come to Greece and become a doormat. Maybe being a traditional Greek wife was off the table. Maybe she couldn't be what he wanted, but my God, she'd be what he needed.

She turned her pillow and punched it and then snorted as she remembered how he'd thrown his mistresses in her face.

Did he think she'd be jealous? Did he think that would hurt her, or offend her?

Of course he had mistresses. He was one of the wealthiest men in the world. Men like Damen preferred mistresses to girlfriends because they liked the power, and control, and they liked having a relationship on their terms.

In fact, it was one of Damen's past mistresses who had

told her father to make sure Elexis was beautifully waxed because Damen wasn't a fan of body hair. The former mistress had been happy to share a few helpful tips…since her father was happy to do something for her in exchange.

Kassiani was up so late that she ended up sleeping in the next morning, and the first thing she noticed when climbing from bed was that they weren't moving, and then as she pulled open the heavy blackout curtains she discovered they'd anchored in another harbor, and she'd been to this one before. Mykonos.

She was surprised they were here, because Damen had said he didn't want to take her to the same spots he was going to take Elexis, but at the same time, she'd really enjoyed playing tourist yesterday and she'd welcome the opportunity to explore Mykonos today…if that's what Damen had in mind.

She dressed quickly and left her room, going in search of her husband, but it seemed he'd already gone ashore. The captain informed her they were to take her to him in Chora, Mykonos, if she wanted.

And since she wanted to go to Chora, they set off immediately.

Damen was waiting for her on shore, and he arched an eyebrow when she stood on tiptoe and kissed his cheek. "Good morning, husband," she said sunnily, determined to at least start the day off on the right foot. "So what is the plan for today?"

"Chora is a traditional Cycladic village, and I thought we should wander the streets, visit my favorite bakery, stop in at some of the beautiful churches and chapels and then we talk business."

She felt a rush of excitement. "Business? As in Greek shipping business?"

"No, business, as in between you and me."

The excitement faded, but she tried to hide her disappointment, struggling for a nonchalance she didn't feel. "Then I'm going to need some serious coffee for that."

They made their way through the narrow streets, turning this way and that, until they reached the bakery, which wasn't up, but down, below street level. The medieval bakery's thick arched doorways, creamy white walls and flagstone floor attested to its age, and there were tables in the back for cozy seating and a delectable display of baked goods at the entrance.

"Best baklava anywhere," Damen said, "but for breakfast, I highly recommend the ham and cheese croissants, or the feta spinach pie. I never come to Chora without stopping here."

They squeezed past other customers to sit down with their coffee and feta and spinach pie at one of the little white-painted wooden tables in the back.

Kassiani concentrated first on her coffee, and then started on the warm, fragrant, savory pie. It was delicious, and the owner came out briefly from beyond the counter to welcome Damen back. The bakery was family owned and had been in business in this spot for two hundred years, with the bakery passing from one generation to the next. After George left them, Kassiani looked at Damen. "So are we here to sightsee, or talk business?"

Damen could hear that Kassiani was guarded, and her voice revealed wariness, too. He hated that he'd taken much of the joy out of her morning, but at the same time, he had to manage their relationship before it imploded.

Last night had turned into a proper mess, and he blamed himself for letting Kassiani get too close to him. She was wanting more from him, not less, and he didn't have more to give her. He'd reached his limits, and she needed to accept the reality of their marriage. Both good and bad.

This marriage was good for her. This marriage gave her advantages she'd never have as a single woman, living in her father's house.

But the marriage wasn't without cost. She didn't have a love marriage. This wasn't a relationship where the husband and wife became close...became best friends.

He didn't want or need a best friend. And he wasn't going to ever be a doting husband.

She needed to accept that this was a businesslike arrangement, a relationship based on clearly delineated jobs and responsibilities.

In the past, he had a contract with his mistresses. The contract spelled out how the relationship would work, and what his mistress could expect of him, and what he expected of her, and how she'd be compensated, as well. It was very black-and-white, and had nothing to do with feelings and emotions. It was a mutually beneficial arrangement that could be ended by either party at any time.

That was what he needed now—minus the clause about terminating the relationship. He and Kass were married. There was no divorce for them. But they could use a contract, something that would spell out needs and expectations. Kassiani might initially object to an agreement, but ultimately it would help her, giving her a better idea of Damen's wants and needs.

In hindsight, he should have had an agreement, or contract, for her on day one. He should have been more organized and logical. If he had been better prepared, last night's uncomfortable scene might not have taken place.

Although, he wasn't entirely sure that a contract would have saved them from all drama because Kassiani didn't play by the rules, but if it would help save them from a great deal of drama, that was a start. Because he didn't like surprises. He hated being caught off guard, and he hated feeling whatever it was he was feeling right now.

What he was feeling made his head ache and his chest feel heavy and tight as if he couldn't get enough air.

He wouldn't say he was panicking, because he didn't panic anymore, but the sensation was enough to make him remember who he had been as a young teenage boy, and how as a fourteen-year-old boy he'd been rendered helpless, and Damen despised the boy he'd been.

Damen despised weakness in himself.

Weakness was pathetic and memories of the past still managed to make him feel worthless and pathetic, which was why Damen didn't just allow things to happen. It's why he didn't welcome emotion. It's why he kept control of situations. And he needed that control back.

He needed Kassiani to follow his rules so Damen could close the door to the past, and keep it closed, and locked. Always.

Kassiani's breath caught as she watched Damen draw a folded envelope from his pocket.

She frowned as he pulled papers from the envelope, unfolding them and laying them in the center of the bakery table.

She forced a smile as she nodded at the paperwork. "So what do you have there? Honeymoon itinerary? A postnuptial? Something else even more intriguing?"

"It's just an agreement," he said, tapping the paperwork lightly, carelessly. "I thought it'd be useful for us."

She held her breath, containing her worry.

"I've always had one with previous relationships," he added. "The agreement is designed to streamline communication and reduce, if not eliminate, misunderstandings."

"How practical," she said brightly, suppressing the urge

to laugh, hysterically. What on earth was he talking about? And he couldn't seriously be referencing his mistresses again, or had there been some significant relationship she hadn't known about? "I'd love to have a look at this useful agreement."

"It's probably best if I go through it with you. I'm happy to read it aloud and then I can explain various points."

"That's not necessary," she answered, reaching for the creased paperwork. "Reading is one of my underutilized strengths." She wasn't just a good reader, but a speed reader, and it didn't take her more than a few seconds to understand what he'd given her.

It was a contract stipulating what he expected from her in terms of *behavior*.

Kassiani snorted as she turned the page, scanning the second sheet, and then the third, and finally the fourth. Finished reading, she dropped the paperwork on the table and leaned back in her chair to give Damen a long, level, concerned look. "I'd love to understand your rationale. What do you think this paperwork is going to accomplish?"

"It will simplify things between us."

"How?"

"You won't be confused about what I need from you, and you won't be surprised by my expectations, either."

She tipped her head, considering him. He was so ruggedly good-looking, and had the most amazing skills in bed, but goodness, he was also incredibly out of touch with reality. "My gut tells me this…document…was something you used to give your mistresses. And I am sure it was *useful* for them. But it's not at all beneficial for us, and I'm not going to sign it because there is no way it would work—"

"Why not?"

"Because you can't tell me what to feel, or if I'm allowed

to have feelings, including feelings of attachment. I'm not a hooker, I'm not a mistress, I'm your *wife*."

"This was not a love marriage. I do not love you, I will not love you, and I will not discuss love every single day."

Kassiani laughed, tucking a flyaway tendril behind her ear. "I only asked you once if you'd ever been in love. Once. And I never said I loved you. I never said I wanted to love you. I merely said I *cared* for you. Frankly, I don't expect you to love me after everything you said. I've accepted you have rocks in your chest instead of a heart. But your determination to control who I am, and how I feel, makes me think you don't just have rocks in your chest, but rocks in your head."

She stood up, leaving the paperwork on the table between them. "I'm not one of your silly mistresses," she said, voice dropping to little more than a whisper. "I don't need your money, either, but thank you for offering me a very generous allowance in exchange for keeping my unnecessary and unwanted feelings to myself. Thank you for thinking of me, and trying to be a good provider. I can respect that you're trying to give me something."

And then she squeezed between the small tables, and climbed the stairs to reach the street, the white skirt of her sundress swirling around her legs, her temper seething, her vision blurred because all she could see was red.

She didn't know how he did it, time and time again, but he had the ability to take a perfectly lovely morning and ruin it. Honestly, all he needed was sixty seconds and he smashed life's gorgeous possibilities in no time flat.

Damen caught up with her before she'd walked too far. "Where are you going?" he demanded.

"Back to the ship. I don't feel like dealing with tourists, or you, at the moment."

He blocked her progress down the street. "You can't just walk away from me every time you don't like what I have to say."

"You wanted a wife, and I wanted to be a good wife, but I realize I will never be a traditional Greek wife. I'm Greek American, and obviously more American than Greek because I wanted to laugh in your face when you presented your contract. It was ridiculous. Damen, you have a problem with control, and I'm not good with that. That was not part of the marriage deal. I never agreed to relinquish all control—"

"You said you'd make my comfort your chief goal."

"Yes, I did."

"Then understand that your emotions are making me uncomfortable."

"You make it sound as if I'm a hysterical female, crying and screaming and having tantrums from one end of your ship to the other. Have I cried on this trip? Yes. But I have only cried in the privacy of my bedroom—"

"It's actually my bedroom."

She threw up her hands in dismay. "Do you want your bedroom back? Would you like to move your wife to a guest bedroom? Is that where your mistresses usually sleep?"

His silence told her all she needed to know.

Kassiani laughed, because it was that, or scream, and she couldn't allow herself to lose control now, not after everything he'd said. "What were these other women like, the ones you love throwing in my face? I'd love to know more about your mistresses, and how they were such paragons of virtue."

"They weren't paragons of virtue," he said tightly. "But they understood the limitations of our relationship and didn't make excessive demands."

"Because they were grateful you paid their bills. I'm sure

you spoiled them with jewelry and trips and clothes, and they probably loved every little trinket and special treat, but I don't care about things, Damen. I don't care about the yacht, or your villas, or your numerous expensive cars. I've grown up surrounded by nice things, expensive things. What I want from you isn't trinkets and treats. I want honesty, kindness, happiness, respect. I want a marriage that is a partnership—"

"I don't do partnerships."

"My father thinks he and you are partners."

Damen's jaw tightened, and his expression hardened.

She lifted a shoulder. "You allowed Elexis to think she'd be your partner."

"Because she would have been happy with trinkets and treats and trips to London and New York and Milan for Fashion Week."

"Because she would have accepted your idea of a partnership." Her chin jerked up. "And she would have been happy with the lies and deceit because she would have been just as deceitful. She wouldn't have been faithful to you, and maybe you don't care. You wouldn't be absolutely sure, short of a DNA test, that your children were your children. And you probably would have been happier with a woman who pretends to care for you, but doesn't. You would be able to sleep at night knowing you got what you wanted— money, power and the illusion of control—while she got what she wanted—money, prestige and tremendous freedom away from you."

"You make me sound like a horrible human being."

"You don't have to be horrible," she said softly. "It's a choice you make." And then she shrugged and stepped around him, her shoulder bumping his chest as she pushed by, before continuing down the street, grateful she'd been to Chora before because it meant she knew how to get back to the harbor and out of these narrow, twisting streets.

The speedboat was waiting for her, as if it had never left, and it ferried her back to the yacht anchored in the harbor.

She kept her jaw set during the short trip, and as she climbed the stairs to the master bedroom. Once there she rang for staff and asked them to pack her things and move her to a different room, one that Mr. Alexopoulos's female guests usually enjoyed.

If he wanted his room, he could have his room.

And if he wanted a marriage, it was going to be a partnership.

She could appreciate the erotic sex, and she could handle his being dominant in the bedroom, but she wasn't going to be a doormat out of the bedroom.

She might not be beautiful, and she might not ever command admiration and respect from the rest of the world, but she refused to feel less than worthy in her new home.

Damen wandered around the charming old town with the whitewashed buildings and brightly painted doors in a temper. He didn't know which upset him more: the fact that Kassiani had moved out of the master bedroom, or the brazen announcement that she didn't need his money because she had her own. He also knew why she'd left the master bedroom—his flippant remark about it being his room had annoyed her—but he didn't understand why she felt it necessary to brag about having her own money. Of course she had money. She was an heiress. The Dukases owned large chunks of San Francisco's waterfront, a historic mansion in the most coveted neighborhood of the city, plus more valuable real estate all over the West Coast. So what did she think she was accomplishing by mentioning her wealth?

What did she think she'd accomplish by throwing her weight around?

After an hour of walking, he returned to the yacht, going to the master bedroom, but she was no longer there. He was informed by one of his maids that she'd changed rooms, taking a smaller room on another floor.

Temper stirred all over again, he descended a flight of stairs, and knocked hard on the door of the guest room she'd claimed as her own.

It took Kassiani forever to open it.

She stood in the doorway in what looked like comfortable yoga pants and a soft T-shirt, her long thick hair loose and tumbling over her shoulder. She looked up at him, eyes wide, expression innocent. "Hello, Damen. How was your morning?"

He had to draw a careful breath to check his temper. He was not going to fight with her. There would be no scene. "How are your new accommodations?" he asked, because he could match her at her game. She wanted civilized. He could give her civilized. "I hope the guest room will be sufficiently comfortable. The bed is much smaller, and there is no private deck, or I believe a jetted tub, but I suppose if you are craving a really long soak, you could use the master bathroom."

"Or I can visit your spa here on the yacht. It's a very well-appointed spa."

"I spared no expense," he agreed.

"I've been able to take advantage of the spa on a daily basis, so thank you."

He gazed down into her upturned face, thinking the softness of her mouth, the pale pink flush in her cheeks and her firm chin belied her inner strength. Kassiani was nobody's fool. He felt grudging respect. "So are you going to invite me in, or do I carry you back to the master bedroom?"

Her nose wrinkled. She appeared to think, her head cocked, a finger tapping her chin. "Hmm. I wish I had remembered the details of that agreement better. Because there *was* something in that document about me being available for sex, on demand, and it was strange, because in the United States we have television like that. You can watch whatever you want when you want. Is that what you are thinking I would be? A wife on demand? With my very privates on demand?" Her brows pulled and she gave her head a faint, frustrated shake. "Maybe I should have paid better attention to that agreement."

"I knew I should have read it to you."

He enjoyed the flash of outrage in her dark eyes. Her eyes glowed hot, the little sparks of gold unusually bright right now. If he had an issue with her, it wasn't with her desirability. He found Kassiani incredibly seductive. There wasn't anything about her body he didn't like. But she was never more beautiful and appealing than when she was unhappy with him. He usually didn't like angry women, but Kassiani in a temper was absolutely arousing.

He was getting hard just looking at her now, and seeing the defiant shine in her eyes and the set of her full lips.

Maybe he shouldn't be turned on right now, but he was, and he wondered if it was because she was the first woman who had ever truly stood up to him. He couldn't even remember the last time anyone had stood up to him. It was interesting. Maybe a little refreshing.

"I feel as if I need to prepare a statement or tutorial for you, my husband, because I am happy to be in your bed, when you treat me as an equal. I am happy to be in your bed when you respect me. But I won't be happy if you treat me as if I am something you own. I am not real estate. I am not your property. I am not a possession."

"You are making too much of the agreement. And there were benefits to you signing the agreement."

"Yes, I would receive extra bonuses with my allowance when we have smooth, drama-free weeks. To receive those bonuses, all I have to do is be compliant, serene and undemanding." She smiled up at him and yet her smile was fierce. "You don't like women very much, do you?"

He shrugged. "I don't like anyone very much."

"What happened to you to make you so…you? There are selfish men in the world, and there are arrogant men, and there are detached men, but you are without a doubt—"

"I really am not interested in discussing my personality," he interrupted, leaning his shoulder against the door frame. "Or whatever you perceive to be my personality—"

"Disorder," she now interjected.

"Or disorder you want to assign me." He smiled, and he could see that his smile infuriated her and his shaft just grew harder. What was it about her that made him want— even be willing—to engage her in these conversations? Because he didn't allow criticism from others. He didn't tolerate dissension, either. But with Kassiani, he gave her so much freedom. He was shockingly patient, and tolerant.

And lenient.

He smiled again, aware that his smile would provoke her. "I really don't care about labels. I am who I am. I am comfortable with who I am." He stopped talking and waited, curious to see what she'd do now. And Damen was never curious about anything. He wasn't curious about anyone. What kind of power did Kassiani have over him?

The silence was thick and crackling with energy. Kass lifted her chin, and looked him in the eye, her gaze locking with his. She was so mad at him, he could see it in the quiver of her lip, a lip she punished by biting into it.

"Invite me in," he said lazily, even though nothing in his

body felt lazy. His erection ached in his trousers. His body tensed. He wanted to bury himself in her soft wet heat and make her arch and whimper and shatter.

"Or what?" she flashed. "You'll reduce my allowance? Take away my privileges?"

When he didn't answer quickly enough, she added, "And just what are those privileges, my dear husband? What do I get from this marriage besides money? Because there has to be something else I get from this relationship, otherwise what is my incentive to remain? I have money. I don't need your money. What I need is something I can't give myself. Have you ever asked yourself that?"

Suddenly the heat in his groin faded, and the warmth he'd been feeling cooled. He no longer felt like smiling. "What are you saying?"

"I'm saying I married you for companionship and friendship. I married you so I'd have someone to share my life with. I didn't marry you so you could constantly control me and lecture me and make me feel worthless. My father did that quite nicely and I've had enough of being marginalized. I expect better of you. In fact I *demand* better."

Ice water seemed to wash through his veins. Damen stiffened. "This is not the way to entice me into your bed, kitten. I do not respond well to demands. Not from anyone."

"I want you to take me seriously. I want you to respect me the way I respect you."

"But you don't sound respectful. You sound like a spoiled, rich woman who thinks she is entitled to whatever she wants."

Kassiani flinched. "You are calling *me* entitled?"

He shrugged. "If the shoe fits?"

"It doesn't!"

"If you say so," he added with another careless shrug before turning around and walking away from her.

* * *

Kassiani refused to give in to tears. She wasn't going to cry, not again today or tonight. But her guest room, even though luxurious, felt like a cage and she couldn't bear feeling trapped so she went down a floor to the living room and dining room and its expansive deck so that she could walk outside on the deck and try to calm down.

Damen had called her *entitled*. Clearly he—captain of his universe—didn't know what the word *entitled* meant.

CHAPTER EIGHT

KASSIANI CHANGED INTO one of her swimsuits and headed upstairs to the pool deck with one of the books she'd brought to Greece with her. They were at sea again and the afternoon was warm, and as she stood at the railing she welcomed the breeze and the panoramic views of shimmering water dotted with distant islands. The Aegean was truly remarkable and she loved how the rich sapphire sea lightened to turquoise and aqua as the yacht approached islands with their shallow bays and inlets.

It was a shame they hadn't spent more time on Mykonos today.

It was a shame that she and Damen couldn't get along. She could almost understand why he wanted a contract… He wanted peace. He wanted undemanding companionship. She could respect that. But she didn't like how he went about it. She didn't want to be paid to be kind, and pleasant. She was his wife!

After swimming several laps in the pool, Kassiani climbed out and claimed one of the lounge chairs, and tried to read, but her thoughts kept circling back to Damen.

He was such a puzzle. Something had happened to him at some point that had made him mistrustful. Something rather terrible.

She didn't know what it was, and she wished she didn't care, but she did. When she and Damen weren't fighting about power and position, she really enjoyed his company. He was smart and driven and utterly gorgeous, which made him fascinating.

And then as if her thoughts had conjured him, he appeared on the pool deck.

"Is this lounger taken?" he asked, pointing at the chair next to hers.

"I was hoping my husband would claim it, but he's gone, working."

"Your husband is working on your honeymoon?"

"Tragic, I know," she answered lightly. "But he's brilliant, and really successful, so I try to be understanding."

"Is that so?"

"Yes, and please don't tell him, because it will only upset him, but I like him." She smiled wryly. "Do you still want the lounge chair?"

Damen smiled crookedly, and creases fanned from his gray eyes and he looked young and rather boyish. "That was a lot of information. I'm not sure your husband would appreciate you spilling intimate marital secrets to strangers."

"No, he'd want to tie me up and maybe put some nipple clamps—"

"Kassiani!" Damen choked on smothered laughter, before dropping onto the foot of the lounge chair. "That should not be mentioned outside the bedroom."

"You have so many rules," she answered. "It's hard to keep up. You might want to have one of your secretaries type them all up and put them in a binder or something. That way I'll have a marital reference manual."

He laughed again and gave his head a shake. "You are nothing like your sister."

"Oh, I know. My father couldn't manage me at all."

"No, I'm quite sure he couldn't. You are trouble."

"I take after his sister. The one that never married." She grimaced. "She was lovely but so misunderstood."

"Just like you."

"Oh, Aunt Calista was far prettier than I am, but I think

we both have the same brain. She was miserable. I don't want to be miserable."

"I don't want you miserable, either." He hesitated, his expression growing sober. "But we're struggling, aren't we?"

She nodded. "And I don't know how to change to be what you want me to be."

"I don't know how to change, either."

She nodded again, and looked out at the sea, still glimmering that stunning blue. Her heart felt suddenly too heavy for such a beautiful place. Damen baffled her, he did.

He could be truly awful at times, and yet she still somehow found him terribly appealing. She wished she wasn't so attracted to him. It would make dealing with him far easier. As it was, her pulse was a little too fast and her senses a little too stirred. He looked so fit and virile in his linen trousers and fine wool knit shirt, the soft fabric of the black shirt wrapping his biceps and muscular chest as if it had been made for him, that her heart raced, the same wildly distracting feeling she had when she drank too much black coffee.

"What do we do, then?" she asked at length, hating the helpless feeling.

"I don't have friends. But maybe we try to be friends. Or treat each other as if we'd like to become friends."

The corner of her mouth lifted. "Okay. Starting…now?"

"Yes, and in the spirit of friendship, would you like to have dinner with me tonight? We'll meet in the living room for a predinner cocktail and some light conversation before a nice meal."

She held out her hand, her smile impish. "You have a deal."

Kassiani dressed with care for dinner, choosing a long burgundy chiffon gown, with black beading on the neckline and delicate burgundy wispy sleeves. It was a dress she'd planned to wear to Elexis and Damen's rehearsal dinner, but with Elexis disappearing, the dinner hadn't happened and the gorgeous dress hadn't yet been worn.

She drew her long dark hair into a side ponytail and slipped on the pair of burgundy heels. She felt very glamorous even before she added some black pearl teardrop earrings.

Kassiani arrived early and, seeing the living room still empty, opened the sliding glass door to step out onto the deck. The sky was a dark purple and in the distance she could see lights twinkling on a small island, and there was another small island on the other side. Beautiful Greece with the sparkle of water and light everywhere.

She breathed in the cool night air, and shivered a little at the breeze. She probably should have brought a wrap. Deciding she'd be better off inside, she entered the living room just as a young housekeeper began to plump the living room pillows on the two low linen-covered sofas. The maid, who seemed to be close in age to Kassiani, then took a soft cloth from her apron pocket and wiped down the various tables, and along the glass-and-chrome coffee table.

The maid startled when she spotted Kassiani, and Kassiani apologized for frightening her.

The young woman answered in broken English that she didn't speak good English. Kassiani switched to Greek, apologizing for not being terribly fluent in Greek. The maid laughed and Kassiani smiled, too.

"Where are you from?" Kassiani asked, still speaking Greek.

"Adras. It is a small island near Chios."

"Isn't Mr. Alexopoulos from there?"

The woman nodded. "I come from his village. Many

of us on the ship come from the village. He is very good about helping us find jobs."

Kass was surprised. She'd gotten the impression that Damen had few ties to his childhood home. "Have you worked for Mr. Alexopoulos very long?"

"Two years. Ever since I finished high school. That is Mr. Alexopoulos's rule. He will help everyone on the island to find jobs, but they must first finish school. He says education is very important."

Kassiani was pleasantly surprised to hear this. She respected Damen even more for stressing the importance of education with the young people of his hometown. "Even the girls?"

"Especially the girls. He said it is vital that women have options." Her smile turned wistful. "But sometimes those options mean we must leave home. That is the difficult part."

"You're homesick?"

The woman adjusted a chair and then squared a large glossy book on the low coffee table. "It's easier now. It was difficult in the beginning. I've learned from the others that being homesick is natural. Some find it worse than others. Some girls, they just want to go home as soon as they can."

"Does Mr. Alexopoulos allow people to return home?"

"But of course. He is the best employer. Everyone wants to work for him, and he finds us jobs, good jobs with benefits and three weeks paid holiday every year. That is a lot for us in Greece. Some people use their holiday to go home, others like to travel. I went to Croatia for my last holiday. I enjoyed it very much."

"When do you go home next?"

"In October, for olive picking. Everyone goes then. It's our economy."

It was on the tip of Kass's tongue to ask if Damen returned home then, too, when Damen suddenly appeared in the living room door, dressed in black trousers and a black shirt, open at the neck, revealing his strong, bronzed throat. He looked devastatingly attractive.

The maid, spotting Damen, bobbed her head and murmured a shy greeting to her employer before swiftly exiting the room.

Kassiani watched her go and then turned to face Damen. Her husband. It was still so strange to realize this man, this gorgeous man, this dazzling man, was her husband.

Kassiani cleared her throat, trying to hide some of her butterflies. "That young woman in housekeeping said she was from Adras, and she was telling me you provide incentives for helping the young people stay in school. I find that most admirable." She hesitated. "I wish you would tell me things like this. I wish you would tell me things about you. I learned more about you from talking to her for five minutes than I learned after spending five days with you."

"I don't like to talk about myself."

Kass sat down on one of the couches, gently smoothing the delicate chiffon of her skirt. "But don't you think it would help *us* if I knew *you*?"

"Maybe." He walked to the sleek bar in the corner, and moved bottles and decanters around. "Can I pour you a drink?"

"Yes, that would be lovely. What do you recommend?"

"What do you like?"

Her nose wrinkled. "I don't actually drink very much. And I know it's Greek, but not ouzo tonight."

"Something a little fruity and fizzy, then?"

"Please."

"Your Greek is a little rusty," he said, uncorking a bottle of champagne and then adding a splash of a dark ruby liqueur. "But better than your father led me to believe."

"I grew up speaking Greek, and I understand it fairly well, but you're right, it's been years since I actually spoke it."

"Did you attend a Greek language school in California?"

"No, Dad's parents only spoke Greek to us."

"I think I remember Kristopher mentioning his parents lived with you for a number of years."

"Yia-yia did. She joined us when Pappous died. My dad wanted them to join us in San Francisco sooner, but Pappous preferred Greece. He said San Francisco was too cold and gray for him."

"Your grandfather was right. It's miserable in summer."

"Not always. It can be nice."

He carried a crystal flute to her, the golden champagne now a pretty pink hue. "Not my memory," he said, handing her the glass. "I was there once visiting friends. It was your Fourth of July. The fireworks in the marina had to be canceled due to fog."

"That does happen," she agreed. "But it's almost a joke to those of us who live there. Will we see the fireworks? Won't we? And if the fireworks are canceled, you just watch them on TV." She sipped from her flute. "Mmm, this is nice. What is it?"

"Champagne with a generous splash of Chambord."

"I like it."

"The cocktail was inspired by your dress. You look beautiful tonight."

The quiet sincerity in his deep voice made her heart jump and her stomach flip. "Thank you," she whispered, touched, flattered. "I feel pretty tonight. Not normal for me."

"I'd like to destroy the person that filled your head with lies. You are beautiful, Kassiani. You are beautiful inside and out."

She opened her mouth to argue and then thought better of it. She and Damen argued too much as it was. "Thank you," she said instead, aware that she was blushing. For a moment she was too flustered to concentrate and then she remembered the young woman from housekeeping. "The maid—"

"Neoma," he supplied.

"You know her name?"

"I know the names of all my staff. I hire them myself."

She was silent a moment, processing. "Neoma says she goes home every October when it's time to pick olives."

"The majority of my staff do. Olives are Adras's chief economy. Olives and honey."

"Do you go home—"

"Adras isn't home."

She suppressed a sigh. "Do you go back for harvest season?"

"I have."

"Do you have your own groves?"

He hesitated. "I own all the groves on Adras."

"All?"

"I essentially own Adras."

"What does *essentially own* mean?"

"I bought the island."

"Can you do that?"

He shrugged. "It was privately owned before, so it was a straightforward purchase, but over time, I've complicated things by encouraging the village to grow, and the people to assert themselves in terms of commerce. I thought it would be healthier for the people of Adras to have true economic independence. So while many on the island do work for me, they also have other options."

"But the main source of income comes from the olives?"

"Olives and olive oil, yes."

"Is there any tourism?"

"There has always been some during the summer, but once summer ends, tourists return home. So a few years ago, a half dozen of my more intrepid locals created a working holiday program, and it was so successful that this year, the accommodations are already fully booked for this fall."

"What is a working holiday?"

"It's where tourists come for our harvest season on Adras, and they stay in one of the small traditional Greek houses in the village, are served traditional Greek meals and exposed to our local culture, and in return, we put them to work in the groves, picking olives."

Kassiani was fascinated. "People *pay* to do this."

"Yes, and willing to pay a great deal for the privilege of working in our groves."

"Do they actually help, or do the tourists get in the way?"

"Probably a little of both, but these aren't the tourists that like being pampered on a cruise ship or luxury resort. They're adventurous and are looking for new experiences, and being part of Greek culture is exciting for them. They have a fair amount of time off, and they enjoy exploring the island in their free time. They ride bikes and visit the beaches, and want souvenirs to take home so they spend money in the village, buying the honey and olive oil soaps and various olive oil products. They also eat in the *taverna*. They drink. They bring life to the little town."

"You don't mind them roaming about on your island?"

He shrugged. "I'm hardly ever there. And I don't think of it as my island. I bought it so that I could give it back to the people of Adras."

"Have many Americans participated in the work holiday program?"

"No Americans yet. Most have been from Holland and

Scandinavia. Americans don't seem to like taking their vacation days, or at least working on their vacation."

"I think it's a fantastic idea. I'd love to do it."

"You're not going to pick olives."

"Why not? Haven't you worked in the groves?"

"That's different. I was born in the village. You're a Dukas—"

"What does that have to do with anything? I'm Greek. The olive harvest is sacred in Greece."

"Adras's work holiday program is for seasoned European travelers who want authentic experiences, not my wife, or the lady of the estate. Women like you do not belong in the groves, or in the olive press. Period."

"Even if I want to help?"

"It's not up to you."

"Why not? Maybe I can't be a traditional Greek wife, but can't I try to participate in Greek life? Locking me up in your villa will only create distance between me and the people who live on Adras."

"As it should be. The villagers aren't there to be your friends, or your playthings. They have their own lives and you're not part of it."

Kassiani's jaw dropped. "That is so incredibly offensive."

"Maybe. But it's better that we are clear on this point now, because I am quite serious about this, and if it's a problem for you, we simply won't ever go to Adras—"

"You have a ridiculous need for power." She jumped to her feet, and set her flute down on the table. "And this marriage is doomed if you think issuing me orders is going to help bring us closer!"

"I don't understand your obsession with closeness."

"It's not an obsession!"

"Maybe because you were inexperienced when we married you don't realize we have a really good physical relationship, one that is mutually satisfying—"

"It's sex, Damen."

"Yes. Good sex."

"But it's only sex. That is all we have. Any conversation out of bed is fraught with tension because you don't want me to think, or challenge you, or have a brain. In your mind a good Greek wife is little more than a blow-up doll—"

"So tell me, kitten, is this how friends talk to each other? I'm serious. I don't have many friends. Is this the way for us to be friends?"

She could see from his expression that he was serious. He really wanted to know.

Did he truly have no friends? No one close to him?

Sympathy flooded her. She sat back down on the low linen sofa. "It depends," she said carefully. "Friends—real friends—are honest with each other. Real friends want the best for each other. Friends understand you, and try to be supportive of you."

He said nothing and her brow furrowed. "Surely you had friends when you were younger, Damen? Surely there were people in your life that mattered?"

"Were, yes, but they're not…there…anymore."

"Why not? What happened?"

He shrugged, powerful shoulders rolling beneath the luxurious fabric of his shirt. "I became me," he said flatly, before stepping past her and exiting through the glass door to the deck.

CHAPTER NINE

DAMEN GRIPPED THE railing tightly, and leaned forward, his gaze fixed on the water, watching the slow churn of the wake and where the water foamed white.

He was tired, and frustrated.

He truly wanted to make things smoother, but he didn't know how to be this person she wanted him to be.

Kassiani didn't understand that his past wasn't a charming fairy tale. Yes, he was self-made, but the climb up had been horrendous. He'd accomplished huge things because he had no choice. If he didn't become someone powerful, someone significant, he would have cracked and shattered.

If he hadn't channeled his fury, if he hadn't been bent on revenge, he might have been swallowed by his rage and pain.

Instead he channeled it, over and over until it became a discipline—head down, mouth shut, work harder.

Head down, mouth shut, work miracles.

Head down, mouth shut, change the world.

Change the world, or at least those in his sphere who were like him—helpless, dependent—so that poor people without choices and options didn't have to be helpless and dependent. And his efforts were making a difference. His efforts had already changed the future for people on Adras, especially for young girls and women who aspired to be more. And his success meant they didn't have to ever be in his position—trapped, cornered, without options.

But knowing that he'd accomplished that didn't ease how unsettled he felt right now.

Damen thrived on challenge and success. He never accepted less than victory. But Kassiani's claim earlier today that she was little more than a blow-up doll rankled.

No, he wasn't comfortable with emotions, but that didn't mean he wasn't trying. Because he *was* trying. It's why he searched her out when she was at the pool, and why he'd invited her to dinner, and why he'd asked Chef to make a special meal. He wanted to try to smooth things over. He wanted to try to make things calmer, but if Kassiani truly wanted intimacy, then she needed to give him time. She wasn't going to get more from him by squeezing him. If she truly wanted more, she needed to push less.

Kassiani sat back down after Damen stepped outside, shoulders slumping, fear enveloping her.

She didn't know how to do this. She didn't know how to be the wife he wanted. She only knew how to be herself—a misfit.

Perhaps if she had more confidence she could trust that everything would be okay, but she had no experience to judge this relationship by. It was her only relationship and she was making such a mess of it.

It would be so much easier if she cared less.

It would be so much better if she didn't want to make him happy.

But she did. He was difficult and demanding but he was also gorgeous and fascinating and maddening and addictive. He entered the room and she felt something inside her light up. When she didn't see him she felt restless and incomplete until she was back together with him.

And maybe part of her anxiety was because she never had been in a relationship before. Maybe she didn't know what relationships were like. Maybe she was the problem… she with all her fears and insecurities, insecurity from never being wanted, never being desirable, never being good enough for even your own family.

"You didn't go." Damen's deep low voice came from the glass door.

She straightened quickly, hoping she didn't look as woebegone as she felt. "That seemed too easy. Apparently I enjoy conflict more than I should."

She was rewarded with a faint smile. Creases fanned from his eyes. "I think you do like to poke the bear."

"I'm sorry."

"It takes two. I'm not one to back away from a good fight."

"Have you ever been in a fight? A real fight?"

"Of course."

"Are you a good fighter?"

"I win more than I lose."

"I don't doubt it," she said softly, feeling a perverse thrill that he could handle himself so adroitly in a fight. "My brother, Barnabas, doesn't win many. I remember my dad once telling him only fools start fights they can't win."

"So your brother has given up fighting?"

"He has people now who manage those situations. He calls them security, but honestly, they're more babysitters than anything else." She looked up at Damen, feeling terribly uncertain about everything. "I don't mean to be difficult. Apparently I just am."

Damen smiled faintly. "You're not that difficult. You are who you are, and I like you."

Some of the tension in her chest eased. "You do?"

"You're my wife." He must have seen her disappointment because he shook his head, his expression rueful. "I don't have to like you. There was nothing in the agreement saying we had to like each other. I like you because I do." One of his dark eyebrows lifted. "Or do you want to argue about that, too?"

She shook her head swiftly. "No. Should we do something else?"

The air suddenly felt electric and he gave her a slow, scorching look. "I can think of a thing or two," he said lazily. "But before I make you dessert, I think we should have some dinner. Chef has set a table for us upstairs in the wine bar. Care to join me?"

"Yes." She rose, smiling. "Absolutely."

Their footsteps were muffled by the carpeted curving staircase in the yacht's stairwell.

The enormous venetian glass chandelier hung from the ceiling, and descended midway down the first flight of stairs, filling the stairwell with glorious gold-and-rose light. The rest of the yacht's interior was sleek with mahogany walls and gleaming wood and chrome railings, and for a moment Kassiani allowed herself to be distracted by the stunning glass artistry and how the golden base covered with countless rose, violet and red glass flowers reflected glittering light onto the adjacent walls and banister railings, before she caught a glimpse of her husband's even more striking profile.

Butterflies filled her tummy and her pulse did a jagged little dance. She was so attracted to him, and found him ridiculously compelling.

He caught her side-glance and gave her a faint smile. "What are you thinking?"

"Just that you are deliciously handsome."

"You flatter me."

"I don't. Women must fall all over themselves trying to get close to you."

Her words had the wrong reaction. His brow darkened and his features hardened. "Some women only want what they can't have," he said. "And I don't care about any other woman. Just you. You are my wife, and I will be loyal to you." They'd paused at the top of the stairs, and he lifted her chin, his gray gaze holding hers. "I don't have a mistress now. I won't take another mistress again. There won't be any affairs. You are my wife and I promise you my fidelity. Do you understand?"

She nodded.

"Good. Because I expect the same of you."

"Of course," she answered, somewhat perplexed by how serious he'd become. But then, Damen was serious. He was clearly scarred from a past she didn't yet understand.

Dinner was delicious, with course after course, from shrimp *saganaki* to scallops and pasta. Kassiani ate until she couldn't take another bite, and then coffee and dessert were served, a gorgeous Greek custard named *galaktoboureko* that melted in her mouth.

Finally she truly was finished and she glanced up to discover Damen watching her.

The dark intensity in his gaze made the air catch in her throat and the blood heat in her veins. Just a look from him and she went hot and molten. "What are you thinking?" she asked, her voice dropping, growing husky.

"I think you know."

"Tell me anyway."

"I'm sick of words," he said.

She flashed a provocative smile. "And I can't get enough."

He made a low rough sound that made her breasts tighten and her skin tingle. "If you're not careful I will have you on your knees worshipping me," he growled.

Her nipples hardened and heat rushed through her, making her prickle and ache. "I'd never say no to you."

The air thickened, heavy with desire. Damen pushed away from his seat at the table, and approached her. "Have I told you that you're not as demure as you look?"

"I do believe you've told me I'm not demure at all."

"Ah." He hit a button adjacent to the bar and the curtains across the wine bar closed. He pressed another button and she heard a soft click, as the door locked.

"No security cameras here?" she asked.

"I've already taken care of that." He took a step away from the bar, pointing to the marble floor. "Come here."

She rose from the couch and crossed the room, going to stand before him. Lifting her chin, she gazed up at him, her eyebrow arching.

"Closer," he murmured.

Her pulse raced and she took a step closer. They were now practically touching. Again she looked him in the eye, and his upper lip curled. And then he reached for her, and turned her around to unzip her delicate chiffon gown, slipping the sleeves from her shoulders to allow the gown to puddle at her feet, revealing her black lace bustier and garter belt. He hissed a breath.

"What is this?" he demanded.

"Something sexy for you."

His hands cupped her breasts and then shaped her waist. "Where did you get it?"

"I brought it with me from California. If you have a beautiful dress, you should wear beautiful undergarments, don't you think?"

"I do," he answered almost reverently, stroking her hips and then the curve of her buttocks. His fingers slipped between the garter belt, and her skin. "You are testing my control."

"And you do hate that," she teased, unbuttoning his shirt, before reaching for his belt, and then unfastening his trousers.

Naked, he swung her into his arms and carried her to the low dark leather couch in the corner, the leather soft and supple as he laid her on her back.

For a long moment he just looked at her, and then he caught her hands in one of his and raised them over her head, pinning them to the leather. With his other hand he explored her curves, and then under the black satin of her panty to the damp heat between her legs. "So wet," he murmured, finding her delicate nub and making her shudder with pleasure.

He straddled her hips, his shaft hard and heavy against her belly. "What do you want?"

"You."

He needed both hands to rip the panty in half, and then he moved down her body to kiss her where she was so warm and wet. He was so good with his hands and mouth that she climaxed far too quickly, and then he shifted his weight, and she welcomed him back into her body, where he seemed to be a perfect fit.

They made love on the wine room's leather couch, and then again later in the master bedroom. It was past midnight now, and Kassiani was trying to decide if she should return to her room, or stay put for the night.

"Stay here," he said gruffly. "I can't have my wife running out of the room after we make love."

"You run out of the room."

"I don't run. I never run."

"But you do leave."

"I can't spend the night with anyone. I don't sleep when in bed with someone else. It's not personal. I promise you."

"Even as a boy?"

"Kass," he growled.

She snuggled closer. "Okay, no more probing questions tonight." She closed her eyes, relishing the feel of his hand as he stroked her back and her hip. She wished he would stay with her all night. She so very much liked it when they were together, like this. After sex he was so calm and relaxed. It was almost as if he was a different man.

She was almost asleep when she heard him ask abruptly, "So how much money do you have?"

Kassiani frowned sleepily, trying to figure out what he meant. And then she recalled the conversation he was referring to and tried to shrug it away now. "Not enough to rule the world, but enough to have a little nest egg should I need to take care of myself."

"You won't ever need to do that. It's my job to take care of you," he said after a moment. "Just as it's my job to protect you. I am responsible for you and the family—"

"We don't have a family yet."

"But we will. And you'll be a good mother."

"And you'll be a good father, too," she said.

He stiffened. "Don't say that. Friends are supposed to be honest. We're supposed to be honest with each other, aren't we?"

"I think you will be a good father. I think you'll learn to open up more—"

"I wouldn't count on it."

"I'm an optimist." She pressed her fist to his chest. "And I'm not giving up on you. I'm determined to get to know you. You don't talk about your past. You don't talk about your family. You don't talk about anything personal, or important, with me. Why can't you let me in a little bit? How would it hurt?"

"I don't like the past. I like the future. It is the future that interests me."

"I respect that, I do, but can't you see that you're a mystery to me? I know virtually nothing about you, whereas you know everything about me and my family—" She broke off, grimacing. "Well, not me, per se, but the Dukas family."

"So what do you want? To tour my village? See the house where I was born?"

"Yes! Yes, please. Are you serious?"

He groaned. "No!"

"Why not? It would be fun. I'd love to see where you were born and raised. I'd love to visit the village and see the houses that you rent to the tourists and the olive press—"

"Slow down." He kissed her, to stop the stream of words. The kiss grew heated, and she was breathless by the time he lifted his head.

His black brows tugged into a line and, frowning, he pushed back her long hair from her face, tucking the strands behind one ear and then the other. "I wasn't being serious, kitten, no, but is that really what you want to do on our honeymoon? Visit Adras? Rather than Crete or Santorini?"

"Yes. It would be amazing."

"It's a very small island, and very rustic."

"All the better."

"You're going to be disappointed."

"I won't. I promise."

It took a day of sailing but by evening they would reach Adras.

Kassiani was excited, ready to see where Damen came from and ready to be part of his real world. She passed the afternoon peppering Damen with questions about his childhood on Adras. She noticed he was selective in which questions he answered. Sometimes he avoided saying anything at all and she'd let it slide at first but now they were within an hour of anchoring at Adras and she still knew virtually nothing about his family.

"Come on," she begged, turning over on her lounge chair on the sundeck, "tell me something about your parents. Are they going to be there when we get off the boat? Do they still live on Adras? Are they even alive?"

He sighed, and dragged his chair out of the bright hot sun and into the shade. "My father passed ten years ago, but my mother still lives in the village."

"What is the village name?"

"It's simply Town, or Adras Town."

"We won't be staying in the village, though?"

"No, we'll be at my villa. But I have a car and we can use that to drive around, so it's not as if you won't have a chance to go to town."

"Does everyone in the town know you're married?"

"Yes. Although some might still think I've married Elexis."

She fell silent, and tried to ignore the anxiety his words created.

"I can see the wheels turning," he said. "What are you thinking right now?"

Kassiani glanced down at the plain gold band he'd put on her finger during the ceremony nearly a week ago. It was far too large but at least it hadn't been worn by her sister. "Sometimes I forget you were ever supposed to marry Elexis."

He must have followed her gaze because he said, "As I said before, we'll get you a proper ring, with a big stone, when we return to Athens."

"I don't need a big stone. This is fine. This is mine."

"Your sister had—"

"Can we not discuss Elexis?" she interrupted tautly. "I realize it's natural to mention her but she's not my favorite person right now."

"Right now, or ever?"

She stared at Damen, her gaze searching. A lengthy silence followed. "We've never been close, no."

"Are you jealous of her?"

"We're four years apart and we have always had different interests, as well as different values. I admire her in many ways—she is the person I could never be—but it wasn't easy growing up in her shadow."

"I would think it's the other way around. It can't be easy being the big sister to a brilliant, precocious younger sister. I am sure she has had to struggle to find a way to be successful as herself."

"She's stunning. People love looking at her."

His broad shoulders twisted. "And I love looking at you."

Heat bloomed within her, heat and a whisper of hope that one day there would be more between them than just the physical. That there would be a relationship. Feelings. Love.

Kassiani abruptly stopped herself.

She couldn't let herself go there, not yet, because he certainly wasn't there. But would he ever be able to love her? Would he ever be able to give her what she needed?

She had things.

She needed love.

Heart aching, she forced her attention to other topics. "I remember hearing that some of your cousins would be attending the wedding, but not your mother. She didn't go to Athens, did she?"

"No. She doesn't like to travel."

"Then why not marry at the church in your village?"

"It wouldn't be proper or convenient. There are no hotels on Adras. There would be nowhere for the reception—"

"Your villa wouldn't be large enough?"

"The church wedding is important, but our family church in the village is humble. And the locals would be uncomfortable with the outsiders flooding the town. My mother, especially, would be uncomfortable with the attention. Far better to marry in Athens and keep that part of my life separate from my mother and those who know her."

"So she wasn't hurt by being excluded?"

"I offered to fly her in, she said no. I offered to send the boat for her. She said no. She doesn't like to be out of her element, and I can respect that. Why make her unhappy? She is a simple woman. There is no room in her life for wealthy or pretentious people."

"So you only see her when you return home?"

"Yes."

"And when was the last time you returned home?"

"To Adras?" He paused. "Christmas." Then he shook his head. "Actually, the Christmas year before last. It's been a while."

Almost sixteen months. Kass chose her words carefully. "You will introduce me to her?"

"Before we leave, yes."

"But not right away?"

"There is no rush. I would rather you settle in. Become familiar with the villa and the gardens and the estate."

"Are you worried that your mother won't like me?" she asked carefully, aware that most mothers did not like their daughters-in-law. Her paternal grandmother, Yia-yia, had certainly never thought Liliana—Kassiani's model mother—was good enough for her son. From the start there had been bad blood between her grandmother and mother, and it had never improved during the marriage, either. Yia-

yia had moved in only after Kassiani's mother and grand-father were both gone. "You do not have to worry about protecting my feelings," she added. "I will not be crushed if your mother doesn't like me."

"Are you truly so unlikable? Do you not expect anyone to enjoy your company?"

There was something in his tone that made her lips twist. He sounded almost affronted on her behalf.

"Would it surprise you to learn that I enjoy your company, kitten?" he added. "Or is that not allowed?"

The corners of her mouth curved, and she felt that whisper of hope return, even stronger than before. "It is allowed. I get fuzzy on the rules, but that is most definitely allowed."

The sun was still relatively high in the sky as Damen's yacht neared Adras. The weather remained almost un-bearably perfect, and the colors of the Aegean were so clear and true it almost made Kassiani's heart hurt. The blue overhead teased the blue of the sea, and in the dis-tance, she could see the dark green of the groves dotting the island. For a moment Kass was reminded of Califor-nia's Napa Valley, and how the grapes rolled up and over the hills, but then the sun reflected brightly, blindly, off the water, and she was firmly back in Greece, with this intense brooding husband of hers who overwhelmed her in every possible way.

Feeling a prickle of awareness, she turned her head and discovered that Damen was watching her, and just like that, heat enveloped her, and an awareness of how he made her feel, and all the ways he pleasured her, and how easily he dissolved her defenses. Even without touching her, she felt breathless and weak. Or maybe that's because she remem-bered how he held her down on the couch and claimed her last night, taking her with slow, deep thrusts before withdrawing and slowly entering her again. It had been maddening and exciting and she'd begged for him to thrust faster, but he'd held off until she was panting and writhing and trembling and only then did he finally let her come. The orgasm had been intense, and he'd held her after, and in that dreamy place between pleasure and reality, she'd felt so close to him, so much a part of him, as if they were two halves of a whole, and whole only when together.

She knew it was an arranged marriage, but the lovemaking and sexual intimacy only served to make her feel more…more of everything, both good and bad.

"We're here," he said, breaking her reverie.

She blinked and focused on the island, and yes, they were close. The yacht was slowing down, too, carefully approaching a narrow dock that extended out into the water.

"It must be quite deep here," she said.

"It's not a good swimming beach, no," he answered. "But there is a fantastic view from the house." He gestured above, pointing to a mass of white buildings set among the green covering the slope. "My villa and pools are just there."

It took a little bit of time for the crew to moor the yacht, and while the crew was tying the ropes and dropping anchor, two open-air Jeeps came tearing down the mountain.

Damen offered his arm to Kassiani as they disembarked, and then thanked the staff before walking her to one of the lifted Jeeps with the large off-road tires. There was no step stool, or low sideboard to step on, and before she could even ask for help, Damen wrapped his hands around her waist, and lifted her into the vehicle.

Just the feel of him against her back, and his breath against her nape, made her breath catch and her skin sensitive.

"Could your mother please join us for dinner tonight?" Kassiani asked as he slid behind the steering wheel.

"No."

"Or at least, could she join us for drinks?"

"*No*. You'll meet her before we leave, but there is no need to introduce you right away."

"But there is! She's your mother, Damen. I'd like to have a good relationship with her, if possible, and it's disrespectful of me not to reach out to her early—"

"She's not going to be a big part of your life, Kassiani, and I'm becoming annoyed that you keep pressing the issue."

Kass balled her hands into fists. "So it doesn't matter what I want?" she said huskily. "It only matters what you want."

"Discussion closed."

She stared at him, hurt, and frustrated, and more than a little furious. What she felt didn't matter to him. She was not a real person, or a valuable person. In his mind she was just another thing he owned…another person to command. "I'm not your employee," she answered lowly, fiercely. "You cannot issue commands. Correction, you can, of course you can, but I don't have to listen, or respond to them. In fact, you'll discover I respond so much better when you treat me like an equal."

"I am not going to do this here," he ground out. "Not in front of my staff."

She averted her head, angry, and furious and hurt, so hurt, so impossibly hurt, and she didn't understand how in just a week he could make her feel so much when this was just an arranged marriage, and it was only a business deal.

Except that maybe she'd forgotten it was business.

Maybe the nights of intense lovemaking had done something to her head, and heart, because he was not a "business deal" to her. He was her husband. He was the man she wanted and needed. The man she craved. The man she…loved.

Her eyes burned and her throat ached. She'd been trying to fight the feelings, but they were just growing stronger.

"Buckle, please," he said as he started the engine.

She did as she was told, but her heart was somewhere in the pit of her stomach. Was it possibly true? Had she inadvertently fallen in love with her husband?

CHAPTER TEN

THE VILLA WAS EXQUISITE, and massive, sprawling in every direction, towers and squares, and courtyards with individual pools and fountains. It was also all new construction, elegant and contemporary without being cold. The white rooms had high ceilings and huge windows and every room seemed to have a sweeping view of the sea. The only color in the rooms were the touches of blue from the mosaic tiles in a pool, to the glazed pottery on an end table, or the woven textile pillows on chairs or the low linen sofas, while outside color came from the profusion of purple and pink bougainvillea blossoms.

Damen gave her an excruciatingly brief tour of the house before leaving her at a suite of rooms that he said were hers. "We're not sharing?" she asked as he headed out the door.

He paused in the doorway and glanced back at her. "I know where to find you every night."

She kept her tone light. "And where am I to find you? The villa is considerably larger than the yacht."

"Staff always know where to find me."

"I suppose that's preferable to your wife knowing."

"You're picking a fight."

She opened her mouth to protest, and then stopped herself. "You're right. I'm just...anxious."

"Why?"

"I want to make you happy—"

"Stop trying so hard. Just let things be."

"And I want to feel like we're family."

"That won't happen overnight. It will take time. When we have the children it will be more natural."

She knotted her hands at her sides, emotions running high. "What if it takes us years to have children? What if we can't—"

"We haven't even been married for a week yet. Why think the worst? It's just going to make you unhappy."

"You're right. I agree." She drew a breath to slow her racing heart. "It's just that I want us to *feel* married. I want us to be a real family."

"We're married. We are a family—even if it doesn't yet feel like it." His brow creased. "This is the danger of relying on feelings. They cloud facts."

"But I feel like you use facts to keep me at arm's length."

"Kitten, you're in my arms all night long."

Her eyes felt hot and gritty and her throat ached with all the emotion she was trying to hold in. "It might surprise you to learn that I hate conflict. I do. I don't argue with you to push you away. I'm not fighting with you to win some imaginary war, I'm fighting to get closer to you—"

"You're closer to me than anyone has been in years. Take that in. Let things be. Don't push so hard. It's not going to help us."

"I want to be your friend."

"Then listen to me. Listen to what I'm saying. I am comfortable with who I am. Pushing me for more will only result in animosity and increased distance, because this is what I am, and this is all I am, and you will not get more from me. Not now, not ever."

They didn't have dinner together that night, and he didn't come to her room. Kassiani was glad. Or so she told herself as she sat in a chair on her balcony, a soft throw from the foot of the bed wrapped around her for warmth. It wasn't a cold night but she felt chilled all the way through.

It was always this way with them. One step forward, a thousand steps back. She shouldn't be surprised. She should be reassured he was so predictable.

Except she wasn't.

The predictability hurt, just as his words earlier had hurt, badly. *"You will not get more from me. Not now, not ever."*

Kassiani pressed her chin to her knees, and hugged her legs tighter, determined to keep it together. She had to learn to keep herself strong. She wouldn't allow herself to be wrecked. She would try her best to be a good wife, but love shouldn't damage, and love shouldn't hurt this much.

What had changed him? What had made him despise love?

Something had happened to him. She needed to know so that she could understand and help him. And if he wouldn't talk to her, she'd find someone who would.

Damen couldn't find Kassiani the next day, and none of his staff could locate her, either. They all could remember seeing her that morning, or at lunch, and each one suggested a place to find her, mentioning the spot they'd seen her last—the dining room where she had breakfast, the sunroom where she'd been reading, the garden with the fountain, the patio where she'd had lunch. Multiple sightings, with the last about two hours ago, so she was around. So where was she now?

He was searching the lower pool and the terraced garden when he crossed paths with one of his gardeners. He asked the gardener what he'd been asking everyone. "Have you seen my wife?"

The old gardener nodded. "She'd borrowed a bike and she asked me how to get to town."

Damen suppressed a sigh of frustration. But of course she'd go to town, and of course she hadn't waited for him, or his permission.

He also had a sneaking suspicion he knew whom she'd gone to see in town. Because why would she listen? Why should she do anything he wanted?

Damen headed quickly to the garage and climbed into the nearest Jeep, before driving toward town, chest tight, temper humming.

He didn't want to be this angry, but if Kassiani tracked down his mom without his permission, she was in serious trouble.

It turned out to be a longer bike ride than Kassiani had anticipated, but once she reached the village, it wasn't very difficult finding Mrs. Alexopoulos.

Kass did have to stop and ask for people to repeat the directions more than once, but everyone she talked to seemed happy to point her in the right direction. People also seemed to know who she was, and greeted her politely, respectfully.

She rode down the narrow lane toward the simple two-story house with butterflies in her middle. Kassiani was nervous but determined. She needed to be a good daughter-in-law. She needed to be respectful and start things on the right foot with her new mother-in-law.

Mrs. Alexopoulos emerged from within, just as Kassiani showed up on her doorstep.

"Mrs. Alexopoulos?" Kassiani asked.

The woman inclined her head. She was surprisingly small, with a slim, wiry build. Her gray hair was twisted and pinned up and she wore an apron over her blouse and skirt. Damen must have inherited his height from his father but the light gray eyes seemed to have come from his mother, along with the high pronounced cheekbones.

"I'm Kassiani," she introduced herself in Greek, handing Mrs. Alexopoulos the bundle of flowers she'd gathered from one of the villa gardens. "Damen's wife. I wanted to come meet you right away."

Mrs. Alexopoulos took the flowers without much enthusiasm and carried them into the house, where she placed the bouquet in a jug she took from a sideboard. Kassiani had followed her into the house, hoping she was meant to follow, as so far Mrs. Alexopoulos hadn't spoken.

The house was just as simple on the inside as the outside. It was the house of a laborer with just one room downstairs with a small galley kitchen on one side, chairs near the hearth on the other, with the round farm-style table in the middle. A ladder in the corner provided access to the second floor.

"Damen didn't come with you?" his mother asked, finally speaking.

Kassiani felt fresh butterflies. "He was working this morning and I had nothing to do and wanted to meet you."

The older woman gave her a long, unsmiling look that did nothing to put Kassiani at ease. Maybe she had made a mistake coming here uninvited.

"How is my son?" Mrs. Alexopoulos asked.

"Well. He works a lot."

"Hmph." The woman studied Kassiani. "You are the other sister, yes?"

"I'm not Elexis, no." Kassiani suddenly felt like throwing up. This was most definitely a bad idea but it was too late to run away now. She'd wanted to come, and now that she was here she had to make this work. "I'm sorry you couldn't make it to the wedding. It was quite nice—"

"Was it? I heard you didn't go to the dinner."

"I got nervous. I'm not comfortable with crowds."

"I don't like crowds, either. Or people who pretend they are something they're not."

Kassiani didn't know what to say to that, uncertain if Damen's mother was implying that Kassiani was pretending to be someone she wasn't.

"How is he as a husband?" Mrs. Alexopoulos asked abruptly.

Kassiani's mouth opened and then closed. Again she didn't know how to answer. "He will be a good provider," she said at length.

"He wasn't cold as a boy. He was a good boy, with a good heart. Very loving."

Kassiani didn't want to betray Damen, and yet she desperately wanted to understand him so she could help him, as well as help herself. "He doesn't like feelings now," she said carefully. "He doesn't want love, but everyone needs love."

His mother's head tipped, her expression thoughtful. "He doesn't know you're here, does he?"

"No."

"Hmm. So you disrespect him?"

"*No.* I want to make him happy. I care very much for him." She struggled to find the words. "I had hoped maybe you could tell me how to…talk…to him. He is very…reserved."

"He doesn't talk."

"Did he ever?"

"As a boy, yes. He was—" she broke off, eyes darkening "—perfect."

Perfect.

Kassiani's heart seemed to fill her throat. She couldn't speak for a moment and she couldn't swallow. She looked away, blinking, fighting tears. She was tired and overwhelmed and it struck her quite forcibly that this visit wasn't a good idea. It would be what Damen called "pushing." It was the very thing he told her he didn't want her to do.

"I love him," she said softly, shoulders rising and falling as she glanced back at Mrs. Alexopoulos. "He doesn't want me to, of course, but it happened anyway. Life's funny that way, isn't it?"

The older woman studied her for a moment. "Ask him about Aida. Maybe he will tell you."

Kassiani was riding her bike back to the villa, silently repeating the name *Aida* to herself, when she spotted a dark green Jeep heading toward her.

It was the same kind of Jeep that she'd traveled in from the yacht to the villa and she had a sinking suspicion that it was Damen heading toward her now.

The weight in her gut turned to lead when the vehicle slowed and pulled alongside her. "Hello," she said to her husband as he shifted into Park.

"Nice ride?" he asked, his bronze arm resting on the steering wheel.

He was so unbelievably beautiful, and his mother's words came to her. *He was perfect.*

Kass's chest squeezed. He still was, at least physically. "It's a lovely day," she answered.

"Where did you go?"

"Into town. Heading back to the villa now."

"I'll give you a ride home."

"It's—" She broke off as he climbed out of the Jeep. She swallowed the rest of her protest and stepped away so he could place the bike in the backseat of the Jeep. "Great."

They drove in silence for several minutes and then Damen pulled off the road onto the shoulder next to a grove of olive trees thick with gnarled branches.

"I don't feel like playing games," he said tightly. "So let's not, okay?"

"Okay."

"Who did you see in town?"

"I don't know all their names—"

"Kassiani."

"And your mother."

He closed his eyes, rubbed at his temple. "Why?"

"Because she's my mother-in-law and it's respectful to take her flowers and pay her a call."

He held her gaze, as if daring her to say more but Kassiani's courage failed her. She did want to ask about Aida but now wasn't the time. Now was most definitely not the time.

Back at the villa, Damen handed the blue bike to one of the gardeners and then walked away from Kassiani as if he couldn't bear looking at her another moment.

Kassiani stood rooted to the spot, feeling sick and sad and dangerously close to shouting something at his retreating back, something that would bring him back but only create more tension. But at least he'd come back to her.

She wanted him with her.

She wanted him.

She loved him.

Kassiani pursued him, catching up with him as he was entering a handsome sophisticated office at the end of the corridor. His windows overlooked the water and a pristine garden dominated by a fountain.

He glanced at her as she closed the door behind him, one black eyebrow lifting. "Yes?"

"I think we should have your mother join us for dinner tonight, and if not tonight, then tomorrow. I know she'd like it—"

"You don't know her."

"But I should, shouldn't I?" She saw his expression tighten and she hurriedly added, "I don't have a mother anymore. I haven't had a mother since I was fifteen. I'd like to have your mother part of our lives—"

"She wouldn't understand our lives. She wouldn't appreciate the…extravagance."

"Maybe not, but shouldn't we at least give her the option? Why decide for her?"

He crossed the pale marble floor. "Obviously you don't trust me because you question every decision I make."

"I just want to be part of the decision making—"

"That's not going to happen."

"But if we're friends—"

"Maybe we're not friends."

"Damen!"

His powerful shoulder rolled. "Or maybe we are, as I'm going to give you the truth. I broke my mother's heart many years ago, and I hurt others many years ago, and I'm not going to let that happen again. End of story."

Kassiani held her breath, wishing his words didn't bruise her. Maybe they wouldn't bruise if she didn't care so much about him. For the first time in forever, Kassiani wished she was Elexis, because Elexis wouldn't care about Damen's past or any hurt he'd suffered. No, she'd simply be grateful for his wealth. She'd love the freedom Damen gave her. She would be able to party and shop and travel, perfectly content with an absentee husband, a man who came to her only when he had a physical need. An itch to scratch.

Kassiani's lips pursed in distaste. She didn't love Damen because he was rich. She loved him because he'd become hers. He, even with his hard edges, was her person. Her man. Her husband. And she wanted her husband to want her, and love her, the way she loved him.

"I respect that," she said carefully, "and since we are friends, I'm going to ask that you at least take time to consider my request. Maybe you don't need a relationship with your mother anymore, but maybe I do." And then she left the room before the conversation took a turn for the worse.

Damen exhaled as the door closed behind Kassiani.

He couldn't do this. He shouldn't have brought her here. Why he'd given in to her requests he didn't know, because it was a mistake having her here on Adras.

A mistake meeting his mother.

There was too much water under the bridge. Too much had happened, things that couldn't be undone.

Even if he could forgive himself, he couldn't forget. He shouldn't forget. And so he wouldn't forgive himself, either.

Kassiani paced her room hot and agitated. It wasn't until she caught a glimmer of the sparkling pool from her bedroom window that she realized an afternoon swim might help clear her head and calm her agitation.

The pool did feel wonderful, too. It was heated, but still refreshing, and it soothed her just floating on her back, soaking in the sun, letting her worries go.

Everything would be fine.

She needed to be patient.

She needed to keep fighting for Damen and their relationship. He was worth it. They were worth it.

A shadow stretched over the pool, blocking her sunlight. Opening her eyes, she saw Damen standing at the side of the pool. He'd changed from earlier, and was now wearing a dark suit with a white dress shirt.

She swam to the side of the pool and lifted a hand to shield her eyes. "Where are you going?"

"Back to Athens."

Her heart lurched. "Now?"

"Soon. I'm having your things packed. They've left dry clothes for you on your bed."

Her pulse drummed. Her stomach turned inside out. "Why are we leaving now? We only just got here."

"It was a mistake to bring you here."

"No—"

"You know I am not a fan of the past. I have done everything in my power to close the door on the past. I only brought you to Adras so you can see where I was born and raised, and you have seen where I was born, you have seen my childhood home, microscopic as it is. You have met my mother. And now we return to Athens so I can get back to work."

"And our honeymoon?" she asked.

"I can't do this anymore. It's not useful. It's counterproductive—"

"I thought we would have fourteen days together." She swam to the steps and rose from the pool, crossing the deck to retrieve her towel and wrap it around her. "You had promised Elexis fourteen days."

"That was Elexis, not you. I promised you nothing. You are not even supposed to be my wife."

She flinched. "Why do you have to fight dirty? It's ugly, and so unfair."

"Why do you have to probe and dig? Why can't you be happy with what I tell you? I have given you more of me than I have given any other woman—"

"Except Aida."

He stiffened, and paled, his gray eyes glittering against his sudden pallor. "What did you say?"

She swallowed hard. "Aida," she said more softly.

"What do you know of her? Who told you her name?"

"Your mother."

His lips compressed. Lines etched whitely at the corner of his mouth. "I should have never brought you here. I shouldn't have trusted either of you."

"She is your mother."

"Yes, and I am her son and I have paid all the debts I owe her. I have given everything to provide for her. She owns my first fourteen years. She cannot have my future."

"She said you weren't always like this. She said something has made you cold."

"You're making this up."

"I'm not. She said I should ask you about Aida—"

"Stop saying her name."

"Was she your girlfriend? Your lover?"

He made a hoarse sound and took a step away, turning his back on her. "You know nothing about anything—"

"Then tell me so I know something!" She went to him and put her hand on his back. "Damen, please talk to me."

"I cannot speak of it. I won't."

"But maybe if you spoke of it, I could help."

"No one can help. It is in the past. I won't go there. I won't open that door."

"And yet, my love, the door is wide open. The past is ruining your present. The past still holds you in its grip."

His back tensed, muscles rigid. "What happened is sordid. It was ugly. When I speak of it, I feel all that ugliness again and not just the ugliness, but the destructiveness. I want to destroy things... I want to destroy people."

"Who hurt you?"

He pulled away from her. *"What?"*

"Who hurt you? Or have I got it wrong? Damen, let me in. Let me help, please."

"What are you now? A psychiatrist? A psychologist? A therapist who is going to sort out all my problems?"

"So you know you have problems."

He swung around to face her. "Is this fun for you? Are

you enjoying yourself?" The savagery in his voice made her flinch. "Do you feel better about yourself now? No longer the pathetic daughter of Kristopher Dukas—"

"Why are you turning on me? There is no reason to make it personal!"

"Because you have made this personal. You insist on talking, and talking and talking even when I'm feeling sick and my skin is crawling with self-loathing, but this is what you want. You want to see me brought down, reduced to your level—"

"No. You're wrong."

"Am I?" He drew a deep, ragged breath. "You want to know who Aida is? I'll tell you. She was the wife of the man who owned this island. She was pretty and spoiled, and her husband was old and she didn't enjoy sex with him. She wanted a beautiful young virile man in her bed, and she picked me. I was fourteen. I didn't want to be her lover. I had a girlfriend. I'd been in love with Iris since we were five years old, and she was the girl I was going to marry. But Aida didn't care about what I wanted. She liked that I was big for my age, and muscular and had a handsome face. And so her husband forced me to go to her, and please her, over and over, because if I didn't, he'd kick my parents out of their house and take away their work and we'd be homeless. We'd be paupers. We'd have nothing. All I had to do was sleep with Aida and make her happy and life would be fine for all of us."

Kassiani had asked him to share the past, and now that he was, she wanted him to stop. She'd tried to imagine what would make him so hard, and what would make him so detached, but none of her imaginings had prepared her for this.

"For one year of my life I belonged to them. I was Aida's pet. The sex was both exhilarating and awful. She taught me how to make a woman feel good. But she also made me hate myself, and others. Part of our deal was that no one could know. No one could know the terms of this arrangement. I thought it was a secret. I was grateful my mother and father didn't know. It allowed me to at least keep my head up because as long as no one else knew, I could pretend it wasn't happening, that I wasn't this boy toy. But I was wrong, people knew. In fact everyone on Adras knew, everyone except my parents. And then they finally found out, just before my fifteenth birthday, and it was Iris who told them."

Silence stretched. Kassiani curled her fingers into fists and pressed them to her rib cage. Her heart was beating so fast. "Did Iris end things with you?" she whispered.

"No. She pitied me. She said she forgave me because she knew it wasn't my fault. But it *was* my fault. If I had been a real man I wouldn't have been manipulated the way I was."

"You were young—"

"Not just young, but poor and uneducated," he interrupted harshly. "I had no power. No control. That was my ultimate crime."

No power, no control. And suddenly so many of the jarring pieces came together in a wild tumult of words and recriminations.

His inability to feel. His inability to be physically intimate without erotic power games. His refusal to discuss the past. His desire for a wife who would be hard like him…

"Do you still love Iris?" Kassiani whispered.

"And there you go, stirring up the past. It has no bearing on the present. It is gone. Dead—"

"Not dead. It's very much alive, and it continues to haunt you even now, coloring every single thing you do today."

He made a dismissive sound and turned away but she followed him.

"Elexis," she said, chasing after him out of the pool area and up the garden path. "You wanted to marry Elexis because she was polished, and hard. You thought she'd be a good wife because neither of you would expect love, and therefore, you wouldn't hurt her, or disappoint her. Not the way you hurt, and disappointed, Iris."

"You don't know what you're talking about. Iris is nothing like your sister. She is nothing like you. She was just a girl, innocent and lovely—" He broke off, jaw tight, expression grim. "Enough. No more. *Please.*"

It was the first time she had heard him say *please* quite that way. He wasn't commanding her, he was begging her. *Begging.*

Kassiani felt a stab of pain. Not just because of his tone, but because of the way he'd spoken of Iris. With reverence. With love. Iris had been his first love and apparently his last love. "You should have married her," she said softly. "You might have had a chance at happiness—"

"Happiness doesn't exist."

"It does. Only you don't want to be happy. You'd rather keep torturing yourself over the past. But you could move forward if you wanted. You could have moved forward with Iris—"

"Iris is dead," he ground out, turning to grab her by the arms. He gave her a slight shake, silencing her. "Iris took her life after I left Adras."

Her lips parted but she made no sound.

"So no," he added, giving her another slight shake. "I don't feel and I don't care and it's better this way. I am happier this way."

Kassiani understood so very much more now, but understanding his secrets wouldn't make them closer, nor would it change the distance between them because Damen was determined to hang on to the pain. His pain was his motivation. His pain fueled his decisions, driving him forward.

His pain allowed him to be ruthless and hard.

She swallowed around the lump in her throat. "If you hated this place so much, why did you buy the island? Why make it yours?"

"It was my revenge on Spiro and Aida. They had overextended themselves financially and were looking for an investor to help them save their business. Instead I forced them out. I took everything from them—their home, their livelihood, their reputation. The family had been here for generations and I wiped every trace of them out." He paused, and his upper lip curled. "It felt good. It felt great. It was maybe the happiest moment of my life," he concluded, dropping his hands.

Kassiani felt numb and nauseous. She reached for her damp towel, tightening it around her chest, unable to think of a single appropriate response.

"You might have excelled in school," Damen added mockingly, "but you know nothing about real life, and you know nothing about me. I am not a wounded man in need of saving. I don't wish to be saved. You see, the only time I feel, and feel good, is when I hurt others."

"No. That's the pain in you, that's not you. You are a good person, and you are worthy of love—"

"Stop it."

"I love you, Damen, but I need you to get help. I'll help you get help—"

"We're done here." He paused and then added even more flatly, "We're done."

They returned to Athens by helicopter. He had a driver chauffeur her to the villa in Sounio while he remained at his penthouse in Athens.

It was strange being back at the villa where it had all started. She was in the room she'd slept in as a guest of Damen's. This was the room he'd come to after they'd married and she'd failed to show up for the reception.

The room was familiar and unfamiliar at the same time. She had changed so much since she'd first arrived in Greece.

Kassiani couldn't sleep, though. Her brain felt as if it was on fire, her thoughts swirling, her pulse pounding. She couldn't catch her breath, not when everything seemed to be closing in on her.

Everything he'd told her explained his behavior, but it also made her grieve for him, and them. He'd been treated terribly—abused repeatedly for over a year—which explained why home was still so difficult for him. She hated what had happened to him, but he wasn't going to let her in, and he wasn't going to include her in his world. He needed his boundaries and rules to cope with emotions… which meant he was determined to shut her out. Keep her at arm's length.

She couldn't handle being at arm's length. She needed to love, and be loved.

Kassiani hadn't married Damen to leave him. She really hadn't.

Her vows had been sincere. She'd wanted to be a wife, a *good* wife, and she had just gotten to the point where she could picture their children—gorgeous children with dark hair, and bright eyes.

And maybe this could have worked, if she hadn't fallen in love with him. Loving him made his cynicism so much worse. Loving him turned the lovemaking into something heartbreaking. To be so close to him, to be possessed by him so thoroughly, while he felt absolutely nothing for her… It made her heartsick.

She'd known going into this that he didn't love her and would never love her, but she hadn't imagined falling for him. She hadn't imagined the sizzling sexual chemistry.

She thought she could handle his moods. She thought that she could remain emotionally detached—and maybe she could have, if the lovemaking hadn't been so fierce, so intense, so consuming.

When they were together, when he was with her, in her, his arms wrapped around her, the world shrank to just him and her.

When they were together she lost track of herself, and her focus became him. He felt like an obsession.

It wasn't good for her head, and it wasn't good for her soul. She felt damaged…hopelessly damaged, damaged to the point where she worried about her ability to survive this life.

And hadn't Damen warned her of this?

Hadn't he said that he'd chosen Elexis because she was hard, and she wouldn't care, and he needed a wife who was as hard as he was?

Kassiani hadn't understood what he meant. She hadn't understood his past, and the abuse he'd suffered—abuse she couldn't bear to think about because it was beyond horrible—but that abuse shaped him, and his past haunted him, and she hadn't been prepared to fall in love only to be pushed away because she loved him. Unrequited love was one thing if the significant other was distant and far removed, but Damen was close, always so close, and his appetite for her only seemed to grow. In his bed, she felt stripped bare—mentally, emotionally, psychologically.

Now tonight, she couldn't breathe. In her room, on her bed, she lay on top of her covers, fighting for air. It had been years since she'd had a panic attack. Was that what this was? Kassiani felt as if there wasn't enough oxygen left. She lay on her bed, gasping for breath, feeling as if she was suffocating, and it terrified her.

This was no way to live. This was not a healthy marriage. Damen was destroying her but Kassiani had been through too much to just wither away and die. Her survival instinct was too strong. She had too much of the fighting Greek spirit to just self-destruct without trying to save herself.

On Adras she'd told Damen that he needed help, but maybe she was the one who needed help. Maybe she was the one who needed a therapist to help her come to terms with her past, so that she could have a future. Right now there was no future.

If she wanted a future, she had to go. She had to leave him. It was the only way. They weren't good together. They just inflicted pain.

Tears stung her eyes but she drew a slightly deeper breath and felt some of the terrible pressure in her chest ease.

Leaving was the right answer. She needed to go. She needed to return home.

Kassiani sat up and stared out the window to the sea. Clouds obscured the moon but she could see a gleam of light from Adras's lighthouse on the water and it calmed her.

She wouldn't go back to her father's house. She'd find a place of her own. She had money of her own now and she'd use the money to start over in San Francisco and from now on, she would be smarter and braver and more self-aware.

It had been a brutal week, but she would feel better once she was back in California. Damen could initiate the divorce proceedings, citing her for desertion. As long as she was the reason for the marriage failing, the marriage contracts would hold. Damen would retain control over

Dukas Shipping. She didn't feel guilty. Dukas Shipping needed proper management. Dukas Shipping was in shambles, and it'd be far better to have Damen step in and save what he could than allow the family business to end up in bankruptcy.

She didn't feel sorry for her father, either. He had pursued this relationship with Damen, offering up his daughters as if they were bargaining chips. He'd wanted the merger and the marriage for purely selfish reasons—he didn't want to be poor. He didn't want to be a failure. Damen Alexopoulos would save him, and his company, and so he brokered a deal that was a travesty in hindsight.

Elexis hadn't wanted to marry Damen.

Kassiani had married Damen to earn her father's approval.

But how could her self-esteem have been so bad that she thought marrying a stranger, much less marrying a man with a reputation like Damen's, would be a good thing?

She felt stupid and pathetic. But now she'd be wise. She was returning to California smarter and stronger, and more self-aware. She didn't care what others would say, or think. She didn't care that people would talk about her, or gossip that she'd gotten divorced just weeks after the wedding. She had tried. She'd truly tried. But she was no match for Damen. She never had been.

CHAPTER ELEVEN

IT WAS STRANGE being back in California.

She'd been gone only a couple of weeks and yet once back in San Francisco, it felt like months since she'd flown to Athens for Elexis's May wedding.

Kassiani didn't even feel like the same person. Maybe because she had married and lost her innocence. Maybe because she'd fallen in love and had her heart broken. Maybe because she missed Damen even though he was not the right man for her.

She knew when Damen was in San Francisco because her father told her. The first time he was in the city, she prepared herself for his visit, getting a blowout to make her hair silky and gleaming, and having another one of those excruciating waxes that left her completely bare down there. She paced her house, anticipating his arrival, hoping he'd come to say he missed her, anticipating his words, wanting desperately to hear him say he'd made a mistake…that he'd made many mistakes…and he was sorry and wanted to try again. He wanted a fresh start.

But Damen never came to her house.

Damen never tried to see her. He didn't even attempt to contact her.

He did whatever business he needed to do and returned to Athens.

Kassiani was crushed when she discovered Damen had gone, and she hardened her heart so that the next time, four weeks later, when he was back, she didn't have such high hopes. She still had her hair done, but that was all, and she didn't walk around in a state of anxious anticipation. But she did hope because she wanted him to miss her because she did miss him.

All she wanted was to hear him say that he'd realized he'd made mistakes and he wanted to try again with her, and then they could discuss the marriage each of them wanted, and how they could meet in the middle.

Or something like that.

But he didn't see her on his second visit, either.

She wasn't in town for his third visit or any others. It was deliberate. As August drew to an end, she told herself she no longer wanted to see him. She wanted nothing to do with him. Kassiani prayed the divorce papers would come soon.

The divorce papers weren't the only thing she was waiting for.

Her period hadn't come. In *months*.

At first, she'd thought she was merely late—it happened a lot with her—and then she thought maybe it was stress that was playing havoc with her system since she'd lost a lot of weight since the wedding, but when the weeks became months and she was fully settled into her lovely house in the Presidio, she couldn't ignore facts any longer.

Something was wrong. And she suspected she knew what was wrong, and once she took a test and discovered, yes, she was pregnant, her dread turned to horror. Kassiani was so horrified she took the test three times at home before going to a doctor.

She didn't want to be pregnant. It felt like such a betrayal to even admit such a thing, but being pregnant would change everything. Pregnant, she would be forever tied to Damen.

Pregnant, she'd given him what he wanted, an heir.

He would be happy. It was what dynasties required… children. Another generation to carry on the family name, to continue the legacy.

Even as September drew to a close, she found it hard to wrap her head around the pregnancy. She'd always wanted to be a mother but this wasn't how she wanted to be a mother.

Single, alone.

Unless she reunited with Damen, but everything in her recoiled at the thought because if they reunited now, it would be only for the child's sake. Damen had made it clear he didn't want her, and while being together might be good for the baby, it would destroy her. Her soul would shrivel up into nothing.

During the long nights when Kassiani couldn't sleep, she didn't doubt that Damen would be a good father, at least, he'd be a good father until the child was a teenager and began to defy his father. Damen didn't like being challenged. Damen didn't like anything that made him feel. Children would make him feel. But there was nothing she could do about that. The baby had been conceived.

Kassiani spent many long, sleepless nights trying to figure out when and how to tell Damen about the pregnancy. Obviously, she would have to tell him. Eventually, he'd need to know and she'd never keep something like this from him, but she had months to go before the baby was born. She was only just entering her second trimester. In clothes you couldn't even tell she was pregnant, her ripe curves overshadowing everything else.

Still no divorce papers arrived.

Why?

What was he thinking? No contact, no communication, no nothing. What did he want from her? Was he trying to intimidate her, or force her hand? Was this just another power play at his end?

And then suddenly, on the last day of September, he was there, on her doorstep, in a dark suit, looking gorgeous and polished and hard, because Damen Alexopoulos was nothing if not hard.

She was shocked to see him and her legs wobbled but she was never going to let him know he still could rock her world simply by standing in front of her, being himself. It was worse feeling her heart race. How could she still love him so much?

"Are you going to invite me in?" he said quietly.

Her anger returned, fueled by love and pain. Who did he think he was, just showing up four months later and demanding privileges? He should have been here weeks—months—ago. "I don't know yet."

One of his black eyebrows lifted. "Whatever makes you the happiest—"

Outrage rushed through her. "You are so wrong, and so unfair, on so many levels," she choked, spotting the large leather folder in his hand. The divorce papers. He'd brought them to her himself. Her heart tumbled to her feet. Hot tears prickled her eyes. "Just give me what you have come to give me, and go."

"No. Not until we talk."

"But I don't want to talk anymore. You've made me wait for months—"

"I was still…working…on things." His lips twisted. "Working on…me."

She stilled, caught off guard by the very American-sounding expression. Greeks didn't work on themselves. "What do you mean?"

"Could we please do this inside? Somewhere more private than Vallejo Street?"

She turned away and walked to the living room, where she took a seat, determined to be calm, and cool, and as unemotional as possible, which wouldn't be easy because everything inside her was going haywire. She'd missed the arrogant bastard so very much, and she was only now realizing just how much she wanted him to still want her. How much she wanted him to fight for her. And how devastated she'd be when he gave her the divorce papers. "What have you brought with you?" she asked tightly, when he joined her in the living room.

"These are for later. I'll leave them with you when I leave."

"You don't want to discuss them now?"

"No." He took a breath. "I want to discuss us, and our marriage."

"Which means, you've come with another lecture on how I disappointed you, and how I wasn't a proper Greek wife."

The corner of his mouth curved, and yet there was no hint of a smile in his cool gray eyes. "No lecture today, sorry."

"You're not sorry."

"But I am. I'm here to apologize. I'm here to ask for a second chance. I'm here to fight for us—"

"Why? When all I've done is disappoint you? I can't count the number of times you told me you didn't even want me…that I'd forced myself on you." Tears filled her eyes and she swiped them away furiously. Pregnancy hormones weren't helping her resolve to be calm and collected. "You were constantly lecturing me and trying to change me—"

"I was wrong. Forgive me. Who am I to teach you anything? How could I possibly teach you about being a proper wife, when I haven't been a proper husband?"

The air caught in her throat. She blinked hard, scrubbing away the remaining tears, even as hope warred against hope. Did he know what he was saying? Did he mean what he was saying? "Then what are those papers?"

"Ignore the papers, please. The papers don't matter right now. The only thing that matters is you understanding that I was an ass, and wrong, and hurtful because I was scared. You were making me feel and feelings confuse me. I didn't want feelings, but I did want you."

"No, you wanted the best daughter, the one my father promised you."

He reached out and lightly touched her knee. "I was promised the best daughter and I was given the best daughter."

"But you said—"

"I know what I said, and it wasn't true. I was hurt and angry and lashing out at you. I'm sorry about that and ashamed. I've spent months—" he broke off, drew a short, sharp breath "—talking, trying to work through my anger and I've come to you, finally, to say that I have never, ever been disappointed by the Dukas I married. Any disappointment I have felt, and continue to feel, is disappointment in myself. I loathe myself for the pain I have caused you, and I am deeply sorry for behavior, and the choices I have made."

She'd found it hard to focus on anything after he'd said that he'd spent months *talking*. Her forehead furrowed as she looked at him. "*Who* have you been talking to?"

"A therapist. You said I needed help, and so I got help."

"You did?"

He nodded, expression somber.

"Why?" she breathed.

"I hoped that if I changed, you'd come home. I'd like you to come back. It's not home without you."

She held her breath as he spoke, afraid that if she made a sound, he'd disappear, and this would all be just a dream because Damen was saying everything she'd wanted to hear. He was saying exactly the words she needed. Was this a trick? Was this real? "You never came to see me on your other trips to San Francisco."

"I was trying to let you be in charge. I was trying to let you control the relationship, but as weeks turned to months, I became increasingly fearful that you truly wanted out of our marriage, and the thought was unbearable."

"I was waiting for the divorce papers."

"You would have been waiting forever. I had no intention to ever file for divorce. You are the only wife I will ever have because you are the only woman I love. I couldn't imagine ever being with anyone else. You are mine. You are absolutely who I want and need at my side, for the rest of my life."

She felt a tremor course through her. His words were powerful and overwhelming. "I don't know what to say. You are so different. It's almost as if you are a different man."

"Words are still not easy for me, but trying to live without you was far more difficult than learning how to be a better husband and a better communicator." He hesitated. "But I'm not here today to try to force you into making a decision that you might regret later. I'd rather we take this slow so that you can be confident and comfortable that I really am the husband you want. I have had months to think about what I need, but it's important we make sure you have what *you* need. With that in mind, I prepared papers that I will leave with you to read after I go, as you don't need me to read anything to you—" He broke off, and a flicker of a smile warmed his eyes. "Because you're quite a good reader. Just know that there are a number of different documents and agreements in the envelope, and each of them have been created with you in mind, so that no matter what you eventually choose—to come home with me, or to remain here, independent of me—you are secure, and protected, and taken care of."

She rose, and he did, too. "I don't want your money, Damen. I only ever wanted you."

The smile faded from his eyes and a shadow crossed his features. "I realize that now. And it might be too late for us. I hope it's not too late for us. I have no intention of letting you go, but at the same time, I won't force you to stay married to me if it's not the right thing for you. And saying that, I also recognize that you deserve more than what you've ever been given and while I can't right all the wrongs, I can make an attempt to correct the balance of power, so the future is nothing like the past."

He closed the distance between them and pressed a kiss to her temple and then another to her cheek. "I love you, my heart," he murmured, his fingers brushing lightly across her jaw, "but I want you happy. You deserve to be happy. You deserve all the joy and the love in the world."

And then he walked out, leaving the leather folder on the chair where he'd been sitting.

Kassiani sank back down and stared at the folder. She'd waited four months for this conversation, and it had been even more wonderful than she could have imagined, except—was it too good to be true?

She hated her doubts, but she was terrified to hope and open herself to love, only to be crushed when he reverted to the same cold, brusque behavior again.

Hands shaking, she reached for the folder and pulled out the various documents. There were three different sets of documents, each with an original cover letter.

As Kassiani read through each of the letters, she discovered Damen hadn't given her money. There was no allowance or settlement on her per se. Instead, he'd given her three different options—all included a hefty stake in his businesses, and none of the options was contingent on her remaining married to him. All three options were still hers, even if she chose to divorce him.

Option 1: Live independently in San Francisco and join Dukas Shipping's Board of Directors, taking an active leadership role in Dukas Shipping.

Kassiani paused, her gaze riveted to the words *Dukas Shipping*. Was he not going to change the company's name? Had he possibly changed his mind?

Option 2: Take a management position at Dukas Shipping, and provide management and leadership for the company, living in either San Francisco or Athens.

Option 3: Work at Alexopoulos's corporate office in Athens in a management capacity, providing leadership for both Dukas Shipping and Aegean Shipping.

Kassiani sat back in shock. He wasn't giving her money. He was inviting her to become part of the shipping industry. He was giving her an opportunity to do what she'd always dreamed of.

She skimmed one of the cover letters until she found what she was looking for. Damen's mobile number. She called him immediately. He picked up immediately.

"It's Kassiani," she said.

"I know," he answered.

"How?"

"I have you saved in my Favorites. You're number one."

"Stop."

"It's true. You are my favorite."

She went hot all over, and it was hard to focus when her heart was racing so. "Those options," she said breathlessly. "They're…amazing."

"If anyone should head up Dukas Shipping in the future, it's you."

"When you say Dukas Shipping, do you mean to leave the name in place?"

"It all depends."

"On what?"

"You. If you are at the helm, it should remain Dukas Shipping, shouldn't it?"

"At the helm? Damen, I don't know anything about the business yet."

"You can learn it. You're a fast study. You figured me out in less than a week."

She exhaled softly, her eyes stinging. "Do you mean this?"

"I do."

"What if it doesn't work out?"

"The business relationship, or the personal? Because they're separate, Kass. You can have one without the other. You can choose any option and not be with me."

A lump filled her throat. He was saying all the right things and giving her all the reassurance she needed, but it made her feel worse. It made her feel impossibly guilty. She had to tell him about the pregnancy. It was time, more than time, but it also might change everything because she was sure he'd be upset that she'd kept the secret so long. Telling him the truth might ruin everything now.

Blinking back tears, she blurted, "I'm pregnant, Damen. I'm twenty-two weeks along."

He didn't immediately reply. The silence was deafening. Her heart pounded so hard she thought she might get sick.

"Damen?" she whispered after a long minute. "Please say something."

"Open the door, kitten. I'm still here. Outside."

She raced to the door and flung it open, wiping away tears as he stepped into her foyer.

"Why are you crying?" he asked, drawing her into his arms.

"Please don't be mad—" she choked.

"Not mad." He kissed the top of her head. "Is the baby healthy? Are you okay?"

"We're both good. It's been an easy pregnancy. The only hard part is knowing you were so far away."

He released her, his hands on her shoulders. "I haven't been far away. I've been here in San Francisco the entire time."

"What?"

"I didn't want to be far in case you needed me."

"Damen."

"How could I be sure you were safe if I was on the other side of the world?"

"But you never came to see me! And my father let me think you were coming and going—"

"That was him being dramatic, that was not from me. I never went anywhere. I have a suite at the Palace Hotel and it's where I go every night after I leave Dukas Shipping."

"Did you ever come by the house? Did you ever try to see me?"

"I drove past every day. I sometimes parked across the street just to watch your lights come on and off."

She drew back, feeling worse, not better. "Did you know I was pregnant?"

"I suspected, but wasn't sure." He grimaced. "My mother thought you might be."

"What? How?"

He shrugged. "She's always had a sixth sense about things like this."

Kassiani blinked. "So why give me those options if you knew I was pregnant?"

"Because you have always wanted to be part of the business, and there is no reason this pregnancy or future pregnancies should keep you from being part of the business. The only reason you shouldn't work is because you don't want to."

"I thought traditional Greek wives stayed home."

"I don't want a traditional Greek wife. I want you."

"What if I choose Option 1, to remain in San Francisco and live independent of you?"

"Then I'd buy a house here so I could be part of our child's life."

"You love Greece."

"I love you and our child more."

"I don't know what to say."

"You don't have to say anything right now. Think about it. Take time. In fact, take a lot of time. Just allow me to woo you and court you, and spoil you. Let me show you that I can be a good husband. Let me prove to you that I can be trusted."

Her heart ached. "It's been a bumpy four months."

"Very bumpy. And it's my fault—"

"No. It's mine. You were promised the best daughter—"

"And I married the best daughter," he said fiercely. "You were the best and only option for me. You and your strength and your courage helped me confront a past that has kept me from living, and loving, and I wouldn't be here, who I am now, if it wasn't for you being you. I love you, Kassiani, and I will love you for as long as we both shall live."

* * *

He did woo her properly, too, taking her out to dinners and the theater, and even to an American football game, which neither of them enjoyed very much, but Damen had reserved a whole luxury box and they ended up sitting at the back, kissing and talking, and it was there that Kassiani asked him about Iris, and his parents.

"I don't understand why you blame your parents for what happened to you when you were a boy," she said softly, uncertainly, "unless it's because they couldn't protect you—"

"I don't blame them, at all."

"But you don't…like…your mother?"

"Dislike my mother? No! Whatever gave you that idea?"

"Because you don't see her and she said you've changed, and become hard—"

"Not toward her, kitten. But, yes, I changed. And it isn't easy seeing her, knowing that she refuses to let me buy her a nice house, or make her more comfortable, and a son is supposed to provide for his mother, but she's stubborn and insists on living as she always has."

"So you're not punishing her?"

"Is that what you thought?"

Her shoulders lifted and fell. "I thought because of Iris, you maybe…blamed them…"

"No. I don't blame them in any way for what happened. They were victims, too. And I would give anything to have my mother come to Athens, and be part of my life there. But so far, she's stubborn and has refused my invitations."

"And you struggle with going to Adras."

He nodded. "Our stalemate, yes."

She processed this for a moment. "And Iris? You've blamed yourself for her death, too, haven't you?"

He nodded again, his strong jaw flexing.

"Do you know why she took her life? Did you two have a fight?"

"No. But I've had plenty of time to think about that as well, and the only thing I can come up with is that she felt betrayed by me after I left Adras."

"Why? Was she pregnant?"

"No! But we'd always talked about our future and how we were going to marry and then I left, and I never looked back."

"A year after I left, she died."

Kassiani squeezed his hand. "You do know that you weren't responsible—"

"She'd reached out to me, a number of times, writing letters, long letters. I never answered them. I never—" He broke off. "I did fail her. I know I did. But I thought I was doing her a favor. I thought she'd be happier without me. I was so damaged at that point. I was not the boy she'd loved."

"And you blamed yourself all these years."

Kassiani reached up, her hand lightly cupping his jaw with just a hint of rasp from his beard. "No more guilt, no more blame," she whispered, kissing him. "No more looking back."

"I love you."

"And I love you, my husband."

After a month and a half of dating her husband, Kassiani chose Option 3, and they were now back in Greece, in time for her third trimester. And while Greece wasn't yet home, she felt comfortable there because Damen made everything feel right. Wherever he was, she wanted to be.

She went into the corporate office with him each day, and he kissed her goodbye at the elevator and she went to her office while he went to his. She worked closely with one of his managers, learning the ropes and everything she could about the shipping industry. Some of the men she worked with were crusty and unhelpful, while others were delighted that a member of the Dukas shipping family had joined Aegean's team.

The weeks leading up to the new year were passing so quickly now. In a little over a month the baby would be born.

After work one evening, Damen drove her to a north Athens suburb to show her a house that had recently been built.

"It literally just came on the market today," he said, as the huge gates swung open and he headed up the long private drive. "It was a custom build and the owner is deeply in debt and is desperate to offload it. I know you prefer older architecture, but the house is on three acres, in a great location and has fantastic views. The only thing we would need to do is buy furniture and prepare the nursery."

He rounded the corner and the coastline came into view, along with the dazzling blue sea.

"How many acres did you say?" she asked.

"Three."

"Perfect. Yes. Buy it."

"You haven't even seen the house yet. You might hate it."

"We can fix it."

He parked and turned to look at her. "I don't want you having to worry about anything. I just want you to relax."

"I'm relaxed."

"And happy."

It felt as if she'd swallowed the sun. Everything within her glowed warm and bright. "I'm unbearably happy, Damen."

He smiled and leaned toward her, kissing her. "Marry me, Kassiani."

She kissed him back. "We're already married, my love."

"But let's do it again. Because this time it's a love marriage. I need you to know—"

"I know."

"I need the world to know."

"Who cares what the world thinks?"

His smile was crooked. "Maybe I just want to show you off. Maybe I just feel like celebrating because I have the most beautiful, brilliant wife, and we're going to have a baby soon."

She couldn't help smiling back. How could she not when the ball of happiness inside her shone bigger and brighter? "You are sleeping with me every night."

"All night. Now that I have you back in my bed, I'm not going anywhere."

She laughed, because yes, that was true. He did stay all night with her now. He'd stopped leaving her room—their room—after lovemaking. Damen slept touching her, a hand always near the small of her back.

She liked it.

She loved him.

Desperately.

EPILOGUE

THE VOW RENEWAL took place on New Year's Eve.

She wore a Grecian-style wedding dress, a simple one-shoulder gown in a gorgeous creamy white. Her long dark hair was loosely pinned up with a delicate antique wreath of gold leaves on top of the gleaming dark curls.

Kassiani was just four weeks from giving birth and she felt huge, but also blissfully happy. Damen came to check on her just before the ceremony began. "How are you feeling?" he asked.

"I'm good."

"You look so beautiful."

She ran a hand over her huge belly bump. "There is so much of me."

"I have always loved every bit of you, even when I didn't know how to tell you."

"The past is the past, my love. It's time to let it go and focus on the future."

"Maybe I can, after tonight. I have made so many mistakes in my life."

"No one is keeping score."

"I have. You deserved a proper wedding and a proper wedding day. I just want the world to know how much I love you."

"I don't really care about the world, and what they know or think. I care about what you think."

"Which is why we're doing this tonight. We're going to have a party with a few close friends and family, and we'll dance and take pictures and put those pictures in an album, and other pictures in frames, so our children will know how much their father loved their mother, and we can be an example to them that true love is worth fighting for."

Her eyes burned and a lump filled her throat. "I had no idea I'd married such a romantic."

"I adore you, my wife, my heart, my life. I adore you and am grateful for every day with you."

The ceremony went off without a hitch, as did the elegant, intimate reception at the Dionysus Restaurant. The restaurant overlooked the sacred rock of the Acropolis and the Odeon of Herodes Atticus, and both were illuminated at night.

Kass thought there was something profoundly spiritual about dining and dancing with the Acropolis in the background, and the evening was made perfect by having a few of their respective families there. Her father had flown into Athens, and Mrs. Alexopoulos had traveled by ship. Mrs. Alexopoulos had made Kassiani's bouquet, adding bits of olive branches from the groves on Adras, the olive branches for peace. And love. It was perfect. Kassiani had found her home.

And when Kassiani went into labor two weeks later, Damen was there at her side. Her father sent flowers but Mrs. Alexopoulos returned, anxious to provide help.

Damen had been worried that Kassiani wouldn't want his mother in the house, but Mrs. Alexopoulos wasn't one of those critical, interfering mothers-in-law, but an unending source of wisdom and encouragement.

Kassiani felt grateful to have a husband who loved her so much that he was willing to fight for her, and them, and a doting grandmother for her baby boy. Their baby boy, their son Alesandro, a symbol of their love, and a commitment to the future.

As winter shifted to spring, Kassiani looked forward to

returning to the company office on a part-time basis. She enjoyed the work, but adored her son, and was thankful she didn't have to choose between them.

The past year hadn't been easy. Both she and Damen had fought hard for their marriage and fought hard for their love. But wasn't that the true definition of family?

Families fought for each other, not against each other.

Love healed, and love hoped, and love endured.

She hadn't always made the right choices, and yet she'd never given up on him. And just when she didn't think she could fight anymore for them, Damen had shocked her by coming through, by choosing to fight for her, for them, for the happiness they all desperately needed.

Dreams really did come true.

* * * * *

COMING SOON!

We really hope you enjoyed reading this book. If you're looking for more romance, be sure to head to the shops when new books are available on

Thursday 11ᵗʰ July

To see which titles are coming soon, please visit

millsandboon.co.uk/nextmonth